ABDUCTION

WOODLAWN MIDDLE SCHOOL
6362 RFD Gilmer RD.
Long Grove, IL 60047
(847) 949-8043

**Other books by Rodman Philbrick
and Lynn Harnett:**

VISITORS

Book I: Strange Invaders
Book II: Things
Book III: Brain Stealers

THE WEREWOLF CHRONICLES

Book I: Night Creature
Book II: Children of the Wolf
Book III: The Wereing

THE HOUSE ON CHERRY STREET

Book I: The Haunting
Book II: The Horror
Book III: The Final Nightmare

Other books by Rodman Philbrick:

Freak the Mighty
The Fire Pony
Max the Mighty

ABDUCTION

Rodman Philbrick and Lynn Harnett

SCHOLASTIC INC.
New York Toronto London Auckland Sydney

If you purchased this book without a cover, you should be aware
that this book is stolen property. It was reported as "unsold and
destroyed" to the publisher, and neither the author nor the publisher has received any payment for this "stripped book."

No part of this publication may be reproduced in whole or in part,
or stored in a retrieval system, or transmitted in any form or by
any means, electronic, mechanical, photocopying, recording, or
otherwise, without written permission of the publisher. For information regarding permission, write to Scholastic Inc., Attention: Permissions Department, 555 Broadway, New York, NY
10012.

ISBN 0-590-34808-6

Copyright © 1998 by Rodman Philbrick and Lynn Harnett.
All rights reserved. Published by Scholastic Inc.
SCHOLASTIC and logos are trademarks and/or registered
trademarks of Scholastic Inc.

12 11 10 9 8 7 6 5 4 3   0 1 2 3/0

Printed in the U.S.A.
First Scholastic printing, July 1998

*To the real Luke
and the real Mandy
wherever they are*

Chapter One

Matt noisily slurped up the last of his soda through the straw, then whirled and tossed the big cup at the trash can across the pizza shop's parking lot.

"Way to go, bonehead," jeered Billy when the cup bounced off the rim and fell to the ground.

"The wind caught it," Matt protested.

"Yeah, right," Billy taunted him. "You couldn't sink a boat with a hole in it."

"Yeah?"

"Yeah!"

Luke Ingram sighed and pushed himself up off the low wall that bordered the side of the parking lot. Billy and Matt were his buds, but lately it seemed like everybody — including himself — kept doing and saying the same things over and over.

School had been out less than a week, and already he was bored out of his skull.

"Later, guys," Luke said, hitching his hands into his jeans pockets as Matt trotted across the lot and picked up his cup to throw again. "I'm out of here."

Billy and Matt both stopped, and turned and looked at him in surprise.

Matt had grown a lot during this past year, when they'd all turned seventeen. He looked like a clumsy bear in his baggy clothes. In contrast, Billy was much smaller and his new spiky haircut made him look like a runt porcupine — which was not something Luke would ever tell him.

Luke wondered what he looked like to them. Too skinny probably, with an oversized head that didn't correspond to brain size.

"Hey, it's only ten o'clock," Matt said.

"Don't be a wuss, Luke," Billy razzed him. "Let's go over to the cafe, see who's around."

For a moment Luke wavered. The Upside Cafe had only been open six months and it was the hottest new hangout in Greenfield. Mandy might be there. Something might be happening. If he went home now, he'd miss it.

Then boredom settled over him once again, like a black emptiness stretching as far as he could see. *Nothing* ever happened in this dumb town.

"Nah. I'm out of here. See you guys tomorrow at the quarry." He turned away, and started up Main Street toward home. "It's supposed to be eighty degrees," he called over his shoulder. "Maybe we can go swimming."

Billy yelled something, but Luke tuned him out. He trudged past closed-up shops, his reflection flickering like a ghost in the dark storefront windows.

In the three blocks it took to reach downtown Greenfield's outskirts, not a single car passed him. "They ought to rename this place Deadsville," Luke muttered to himself.

But instead of turning down Broom Street where he lived, Luke kept walking. His parents would have a stroke if he got home this early. They'd wonder what was wrong. His mother would start fussing, peering at him like she was afraid of what she might see.

Luke sighed. Actually his 'rents were pretty cool most of the time. But lately they'd been getting weird. Like they didn't trust him. Like they blamed him for stuff they heard on the news. *Teen Psychos Run Wild. Honor Student Terrorizes Neighborhood.*

He'd tried arguing. "Mom, Dad, get real. I'm not going to steal a car. I'm not going to smoke crack. And there's only a very small chance I'll get the whole cheerleading squad pregnant!"

His mom looked shocked and his dad just said, "Don't talk to your mother that way."

Of course, Luke knew the *real* reason his parents were acting this way. It was all Jeff's fault.

Lately, Luke's fifteen-year-old brother had turned sullen, shaved his head, and got into body piercing and tattoos. He hardly ever opened his mouth anymore except to eat, and when he did say something, it was always sarcastic.

You could hardly blame the 'rents for being frantic. Whatever happened to the worshipful younger brother who used to follow him around like a shadow? How had that basically cool kid turned into a sullen skinhead?

Luke shrugged disgustedly, walking on until the neat streets with their neat houses petered out at the old, disused railroad tracks. He crossed the tracks and left Main Street, climbing a rutted path that led to Old High Street.

Before the highway went in, Old High Street had been the main route between towns. No one used it anymore. The road hadn't even been paved since the Dark Ages before Luke was born.

The high-tension power lines were still strung along the road though, the thick wires buzzing like a private telegraph. The tall aluminum poles towered over the dark landscape —

scraggly woods and the rocky humped hills behind the old limestone quarry.

The quarry pool had been enlarged, landscaped, and turned into a park and picnic area with an entrance on Main Street. But you couldn't see any of that from where Luke was standing.

There were no streetlights. The pale half-moon looked brighter here away from town, but it didn't shed much light. And the only sound was the electric sputter of the wires.

The wires dominated Old High Street. Encased in thick rubber, the heavy cables traveled in six separate tiers, carried on pylons four feet thick at the base, rising sixty or seventy feet in the air. Each pylon bristled with insulators.

Nothing could contain the singing of the deadly current they carried.

Tonight, for some reason, the sound stirred the fine hairs at the base of Luke's neck.

It was a good place to brood.

The poles marched to the top of a low rise, where they butted up against another set of massive pylons crossing east-west. The furious sputter of their meeting and the thick tangle of lines reminded Luke of a nest of writhing black snakes.

The electrical noise seemed especially intense tonight.

As Luke neared the top of the rise, a sharp crackle made him jerk his head up. He jumped as a sudden shower of sparks exploded off the junction.

That wasn't supposed to happen, was it?

Suddenly everything went quiet.

Total silence.

Weird. He couldn't hear the cars from the overpass. Nothing, not even the buzz of the wires. It was like somebody had turned down the volume control.

A wind sprang up, a gust that nearly pushed Luke off the road. Then it died. The air was completely still. And suddenly as frigid and cold as the grave.

Luke felt his hair stand on end — from the cold? From the electricity in the air? All at once he felt afraid.

He looked up. A small sound escaped his tightening throat. Suddenly all the air was sucked from his lungs. He was frozen in place, feet welded to the ground.

Slowly the stars winked out of the sky one by one. The moon disappeared. The sky turned black.

Every muscle shrieked to run. But Luke couldn't move.

He stood paralyzed as the absolute darkness descended over him like a huge hungry mouth.

Chapter Two

It was a groan that woke her. She emerged like she was swimming up out of some deep, dark hole. Her mind felt sluggish, drained.

With dawning horror, she realized she didn't know who she was.

Her hands pushed against rough boards. Boards? But she was in bed — wasn't she? Cool air brushed her face.

Fear batted the inside of her skull like a moth against a window.

Then, with a rush that made her head ache, awareness flooded back.

She was Mandy Durgin, seventeen, and she lived at 12 Hopewell Terrace. And she had gone up to bed to read at ten o'clock. That was the last thing she remembered.

The headache receded, but the fear grew. Because she wasn't in bed. She was outdoors. Lying on her own front porch. Dressed in nothing but the oversize T-shirt and panties she wore to bed.

Ice congealed around her heart. How had she gotten here?

Mandy jumped up. Suddenly she needed to get inside the house — now. Something was coming to get her — she knew it instinctively. Something awful, something unknowable, something from the deepest, darkest corner of her nightmares.

She bolted for the front door. Locked. A scream started from deep inside her as panic hammered at her ribs. Mandy bit her lip in the effort to hold the scream back.

Her house was dark. She had no idea what time it was. Every house on the street was dark.

If she woke her parents, she would have to explain all this — and she didn't have a clue. No idea of how she'd gotten here, or why she was so terrified. Mandy shuddered. She struggled to get her ragged breathing under control.

The basement. There was a key by the bulkhead. She could get in through the basement.

Mandy turned her back on the house and crossed the porch, shivering in her thin T-shirt. She started down the steps to the front walk.

Halfway down she stopped, clutching the rail, unable to take another step.

Someone — some *thing* — was watching her.

Something was waiting for her to step off the porch steps. She could feel the eager eyes. Predatory eyes.

She scanned the street anxiously. Nothing moved. But there were so many bushes and trees.

Anyone, or anything, could be hiding out there, staring from the inky shadows. Motionless under the Hudsons' big maple or crouched down beside the Browns' hedge.

Mandy shivered convulsively. She felt so exposed.

Invisible eyes seemed to bore right through her, as if the watcher could see her thumping heart and pulsing arteries. She felt like a bug pinned under a microscope.

The panicky feeling worked up into her throat again. Mandy swallowed hard and forced herself to take a deep, shaky breath. Then another.

She had to get calm. Once she was safe inside the house, she could figure all this out. There was a rational explanation. There had to be.

But right now what she had to think about was getting down the porch steps. Around to the basement.

Keeping her thoughts focused on moving, Mandy crept down the steps.

"Nobody is out there," she told herself. "Nobody but me."

She stepped down to the ground.

Instantly a black shape shot out from behind the bushes at the side of the house.

It leaped into the air, straight for her.

Chapter Three

Luke's arms and legs flailed in panic. He was falling, plummeting through total blackness. He didn't know where he was or how long he had been falling.

His hands worked convulsively. But there was nothing to grip. Faster and faster he hurtled, downward through a bottomless abyss.

And then suddenly —

He landed. His body jerked. His breath slammed in his chest like something solid. His head was spinning.

He felt something soft and springy under him. Something familiar. As his whirling brain slowed, objects came into view. His desk, cluttered with junk; his chair, piled with clothes.

With a start Luke realized he was in his own room, in his own bed.

Relief flooded his dazed mind. It had all been

a dream. Just a particularly horrible nightmare.

But something wasn't right.

Luke looked down at himself and realized he was fully clothed — right down to his sneakers. He couldn't remember getting into bed. He couldn't remember coming home.

He sat up and held his head in his hands, struggling to remember. The effort was like pushing through a net of spiderwebs.

Dimly he remembered the crackling wires, the moon vanishing, the sky blotting out. Then nothing. Just nothing. The last thing he remembered was . . . nothing.

He sat for a moment, searching his brain. But it was like there was a brick wall in the center of his head. No, not brick. Steel. Like a solid steel door had slammed shut, closing off his memory of what had happened out on Old High Street under the high-tension wires.

He shook his head to clear it and turned to look at the luminous dial of his clock. Two A.M. He'd lost four whole hours! But how could he not remember getting home?

And then something else struck him.

Voices downstairs. At two in the morning.

Listening, he realized the voices belonged to his parents. They sounded frantic, urgent, like something bad had happened. Jeff? Had his brother Jeff finally gotten in real trouble?

Pushing his own worries aside, Luke left his room and crept downstairs.

Every light in the house was on.

Luke could hear his father on the phone. His mom caught sight of him when he was halfway down the stairs. Her eyes went wide and then — amazingly — she burst into tears!

Luke's father whirled at his wife's cry. He gave his son a ferocious look then spoke quickly into the phone. "Never mind. Sorry to bother you, officer. He's just come home."

Dad dropped the phone and took two long strides across the room so he was right in Luke's face.

"Where have you been?" he demanded. "Did you really think you could get away with sneaking back in through your bedroom window?"

"But my room's on the second floor," stammered Luke. "How could I —"

"Don't lie to me," his father shouted, eyes bugging out of his head. "I checked your room not half an hour ago and you weren't there!"

"But I swear," Luke protested, "I was walking home. Early, around ten or even earlier. And then it got, like, weird. I must have blacked out or something."

"'Like weird'!? 'Or something'!? Just what is that supposed to mean?"

Luke flinched at his father's scathing tone.

"Way to go, Luke," someone else said.

He noticed his skinhead brother, Jeff, sitting across the room, smirking, the ring in his nose winking in the blazing light. He was totally enjoying the fact that at last Luke was in real trouble.

"Look at me when I talk to you!" their father yelled. "Do you know what would have happened to me if I'd pulled a stunt like this when I was your age? Forget about it!"

Luke flinched again as his father smacked his big fist into the palm of his hand. He was nearly as tall as his dad but nowhere near as big or strong.

"John, stop," said Luke's mom, putting a hand on her husband's arm. "It's late. Luke, go to bed. We'll discuss this in the morning."

His father backed away and Luke headed up the stairs. His parents' voices trailed him, along with his brother Jeff.

"Maybe he did black out, John," his mother was saying. "He could have hit his head or had some kind of seizure. Maybe we should take him to Dr. Fanelli before we jump to conclusions."

"Oh, please, Margaret, you're not going to buy that nonsense, are you? He's obviously lying!"

Jeff snickered as they reached the upstairs hall. "Good going, bro'," he said, like this was the greatest thing since his first pierced ear.

Luke went into his room and closed the door softly, shutting his parents' voices to a murmur. He went to bed but couldn't sleep.

Eventually even the 'rents quit arguing about him and went to bed. But Luke still couldn't sleep.

What was happening to him? Why couldn't he remember? How had he lost four hours out of his life?

But even worse than the black hole in his head was the strangest feeling.

A sensation like a ghost of a memory: a feeling that eyes were focused right on him, studying him like a bug.

Luke kept turning and tossing. He tried burrowing under the covers, putting his pillow over his head. But nothing worked.

The creepy feeling would not go away. Something out there was *watching* him.

Something not human.

Chapter Four

Darker than night, the black shape separated itself from the darkness.

It launched into the air.

Mandy froze, heart-stopped. The dark thing filled her vision as it hurtled straight at her. She couldn't move.

It snarled. The awful noise jump-started Mandy like a switch. She dodged back out of its path.

With a shrill cry the Johnsons' cat landed a foot in front of her and raced off across the lawn, a black blur.

Mandy leaned against the stair railing, clutching a hand to her pounding heart. Adrenaline coursed through her, making her shaky. She felt a giggle of panic rising, but it passed.

She still sensed eyes on her.

Trying to shake off the feeling, Mandy edged

around the side of the house, keeping a wary eye on the street.

Then she bolted for the back. The half-moon was just bright enough to keep her from stumbling over her mother's newly planted flower beds.

Chest heaving, Mandy stopped once more to watch and listen. Nothing moved. Her shuddery breath was the only sound.

Mandy ran to the basement bulkhead. She went to search for the round stone under the bush next to the bulkhead. Her hand closed over it.

She pushed the rock aside and felt for the key that was supposed to be there. Her fingers touched the cool, familiar metal.

Relief flooded her. But it drained just as quickly. The bulkhead door squeaked. What if her parents heard? What if they thought it was a prowler?

She pushed the anxiety away. That was a chance she'd have to take.

Bracing herself for the noise, Mandy hauled open the bulkhead door. The screech of rusted hinges ripped through the night. Mandy froze, looking up at the house.

It was hard to tell how long she waited but no lights came on, no windows opened.

She hurried down the concrete steps of the

bulkhead, stuck the key in the basement door lock. It turned easily. The door opened.

Her knees felt weak. Mandy wanted to rush inside and slam the door behind her, shutting out the night. But she couldn't leave the bulkhead open. Her parents would be alarmed. There would be questions.

Swallowing her reluctance, Mandy forced herself to go back up and shut the bulkhead. But she'd forgotten to switch on the basement light.

When the bulkhead came down, darkness fell on her like the blow of an axe.

It was so dark she felt dizzy. As if the nightmarish thoughts held back in her mind were suddenly whirling free, flinging themselves out to fill up the blackness.

Almost whimpering with panic, Mandy felt her way back down the stairs, clinging to the wall. She pushed open the basement door and fumbled for the light switch beside the door.

But all she felt was smooth wall. Mandy reached higher, then lower. No switch. It couldn't have just disappeared.

Suddenly a thought jolted her. She was feeling along the left-hand wall. The light switch was on the right-hand wall. It always had been.

Mandy felt the ice close deeper around her heart. That wasn't the sort of mistake she made. She knew right from left instinctively, never had to stop and think like some people did. What was happening to her?

Her mind was going. Bits of it dissolving like melting glue.

Mandy reached out with her right hand and found the switch. She snapped it on. Nothing happened. The darkness pressed her from all sides.

Gritting her teeth in misery, she started across the pitch-black basement, her arms out-stretched, feeling for obstacles.

If she could only get upstairs, everything would be all right. It wouldn't matter if her parents heard her then. She could say she'd been hungry or something, going for ice cream in the freezer.

"Ow!" She cursed quietly, rubbing her shin. She'd barked it on the metal leg of her dad's table saw. The pain pulsed red before her eyes.

But the table saw was supposed to be in the rear corner of the basement, not out in the middle of the floor in front of the stairway. It wasn't the sort of thing her dad moved. Too heavy.

Mandy knew she couldn't be *that* disoriented. She had a superb sense of direction. A wave of uncertainty rolled through her, making her legs wobble. She moved around the table, her arms out. When her hands touched the wall, fear washed over her.

The table saw was right where it was supposed to be. She'd been moving in the exact wrong direction.

She was lost in her own basement. Something was wrong with her head.

"Get a grip," she told herself sternly, taking a deep breath. She turned until she *knew* she was facing the stairs. Sliding one foot forward at a time, she moved again.

Luckily her father wasn't the kind to leave things laying around so there was nothing to trip her up. But even though she knew, absolutely knew, she was heading in a straight line, she kept veering into her dad's workbench, which was against the wall, across from the stairs.

"Anybody could get turned around in total darkness," Mandy told herself. "Even me."

But her chest felt tight with anxiety. A tiny part of her was afraid she'd never get out, that she'd go around in circles in this musty basement forever.

Where were the stairs? She should be there by now.

Mandy froze as a tiny scrabbling noise sounded in the dark behind her. At least she thought it was a noise. A mouse?

Or maybe it was her imagination. Somehow it seemed more frightening that she couldn't tell whether the noise was real or not.

Then she heard it again. It was definitely a

noise. Something alive. And it could see better than she could, for sure.

Mandy flailed her arms out wildly and — *bang* — hit something. The stairs! She felt so relieved, she scarcely noticed the ringing pain in her fingers.

Hanging on as if the staircase might move away if she let go, Mandy reached the bottom. She shot up the stairs as if she thought something might try to stop her.

For a horrible instant she was afraid the upstairs door was going to be locked; then she was through the door, in the hallway. Her legs gave out and she fell in a heap on the polished wood floor.

Moonlight filtered through the curtained windows. It made the dark house seem bright in comparison to the impenetrable blackness of the basement.

Mandy sat, too weak to move. The house was hushed. She was sure she was the only one awake.

Cautiously, she let her mind return to her awakening on the porch. She pushed her memory farther back, trying to see how she had got there.

There were the porch boards, her hand aware of splintery roughness. And before that a groan as she had wakened. And before that —

Suddenly her mind spun dizzily. She felt as if

she were perched, teetering, on the edge of a cliff, nothing but a black abyss before her.

Mandy clapped her hands over her mouth to keep from screaming out. Her stomach clenched.

She stumbled to her feet. The house seemed to tilt under her.

She needed to get to her room. Fixing her mind on that, refusing to think of anything else, she lurched down the hall, through the living room, and up the stairs to the top floor.

Everything was quiet. She crept across the carpeted hallway to her room and opened the door. Inside looked normal. The bedclothes were thrown back as if she'd just gotten up for a minute.

Moonlight fell on her parade of little magnetic animals. They marched along their strip of beaten metal sheeting on the wall above her bed. A childhood collection, they only remained because she never noticed them anymore.

The book she'd been reading was facedown on the floor. Her window was open, her telescope set up beside it. There was the usual mess of shorts and jeans, T-shirts and sandals, on the floor.

Everything was the same as she remembered.

Mandy heaved a sigh. She shut the door behind her. Suddenly her legs felt so shaky she wasn't sure she could make it to bed. She started forward.

Her eye caught movement to her left. She jumped, her heart in her throat.

The mirror. It was only the mirror on her closet door. Mandy looked at her own shadowy image. It was a shock to see how normal she looked.

Her long blond hair was matted and tangled and her normally steady blue eyes looked wild, but mostly she looked like she might have gotten up to go to the bathroom or something.

Her T-shirt wasn't torn or dirty, her arms and legs weren't scratched or bruised. Her legs might feel like rubber, but in the mirror they looked as strong and slender as ever.

Mandy felt calmer looking at herself in the mirror. Obviously nothing serious had happened to her. She must have been sleepwalking.

She had never done that before.

She must have had a bad dream. Something in it caused her to walk outside in her sleep. At least she had sense enough to wake up before she got any farther than the porch.

Mandy's skin crawled. It didn't matter how firmly she told herself there was a rational explanation. Something felt very wrong.

As if the whole world had shifted slightly, leaving her out of synch.

Mandy turned away from the tall, slim figure in the mirror and got into bed. She told herself it was only natural to feel disturbed and out of it after such a weird experience. She told herself she'd feel better in the morning. But she didn't really believe it.

There was a sick feeling of dread coiled in her stomach. She felt as if something bad had happened but worse was coming.

Mandy glanced at the luminous dial on her clock radio.

It was 2:30 A.M.

How long had she been outside? What had happened to her in those four and a half hours?

Mandy clutched her blanket. She had to put this doom-type thinking out of her mind. She was scaring herself for no good reason.

She was a rational person. Tomorrow everything would look different. Meanwhile she had to focus on something else. Something good.

Think about swimming tomorrow at the quarry. How great the water would feel.

Think about that cute boy who always seemed to be around lately. Luke. Too bad he was so shy.

Not that he was all that good-looking. His nose was too big and his dark, curly hair was too wiry.

But there was something so—*there*—about

him. He wasn't always posing and checking himself out like other boys.

And he had the most expressive, warmest, brown eyes she had ever encountered.

Mandy closed her eyes. But it wasn't Luke's angular face and warm brown eyes that materialized in her mind.

Instead, the eyes that bored intently into hers were gray, like dirty ice. Their expression was cold and so evil she felt paralyzed.

The face filled her mind. It pressed so close she could see every black-pitted pore. Lank, greasy hair brushed her forehead.

It was a familiar face. Mandy squirmed away in terror.

But she was pinned in place.

The black abyss rushed up around her. It sucked her down.

She felt its clammy force envelop her, choking off her scream.

Then the blackness invaded her mind, and that was the last she knew.

Chapter Five

Luke waited until his dad had gone to work before he got up. Usually he bounced out of bed, full of energy as long as it wasn't a school day.

But this morning his arms and legs felt encased in lead. Pulling on swim trunks and a T-shirt was a struggle. His mind kept going blank on him. He kept forgetting what he was doing.

"I hope I'm not coming down with something," he muttered to himself.

His mother echoed those words when he went down to breakfast.

First she tried asking him about last night. "Are you sure you can't remember anything?" she pressed. "Did you fall, maybe? Hit your head?"

It seemed like her words were coming at him from a long ways away. He knew it was taking him too long to answer. But he couldn't help it. He was operating in a thick, soupy fog. As if his mind wasn't entirely his own.

"Could be, Mom," he said finally. "I was walking on Old High Street. It's so dark there, and there's all kinds of potholes. Maybe I did fall."

She fussed over him, feeling his head for lumps, until Luke felt like he couldn't stand it anymore. He was going to explode.

Then she stopped. "I don't know, Luke. I can't detect any injuries, but I'm no doctor."

She picked up her purse and looked at him worriedly. "I've got to go. I'm going to be late for work. If you feel dizzy or anything, anything at all, I want you to call Dr. Fanelli right away. Promise?"

She gave him another worried look before she left, but Luke could tell her heart wasn't in it. She wanted to believe him, but it was hard.

He didn't blame her. He wouldn't believe it himself, except he was the one it happened to. Total blackout. More than four and a half hours subtracted from his life. Like a big black hole in his brain.

And afterwards, that creepy feeling of eyes inside his mind. Eyes busy under his skin.

He grabbed his towel and headed out the door. What he needed was a long, hard swim in the cold water of the quarry pool. That would clear his head.

Exercise always energized Luke. He set off up the block in a slow jog. A good run would get his blood moving. It always worked.

Problem was, he felt like he was running in deep sand.

After only two blocks, Luke's breath was labored. He wanted to give up and walk. But then Sue Ellen came out of her friend Lorrie's house, and the fear of having to speak to her jolted him into a sprint.

His mind flashed on the one date he and Sue Ellen had had, two months ago. Luke hadn't gone out with anybody since.

He had known he was in trouble right away. Sue Ellen had opened the door wearing a short, slinky, shiny dress with thin straps and shiny high-heeled shoes. Luke instantly felt like a major dork in his jeans and blue-striped sweater.

He'd been thinking pizza and a movie. She let him know she had dinner and dancing in mind. The fancy food had taken almost all his money. He'd been so worried about what to order he couldn't think of one word to say. Duh.

Then the dancing. After the cover charge at the club, he only had money enough for one Coke. He had told her he wasn't thirsty.

He also had told her he couldn't dance, but she didn't believe him until he stomped on her shiny shoes, nearly breaking her toe.

Thinking of any part of it — the dreaded date — could still make him shudder.

"Hey, Luke! Wait up, man!"

With a start, Luke realized he was almost at the quarry park. His friend Matt came running up, red-faced and out of breath.

"I've been calling your name for the last two blocks," said Matt. "What are you, training for the Olympics?"

"Sorry. I was thinking," Luke explained. "I guess I didn't hear you."

"Whoa, thinking?" Matt widened his eyes in mock surprise. "I thought I smelled something burning. Hope you didn't do any permanent damage."

Luke smiled, but he could feel it was more of a grimace. His heart was pumping strong and his blood was zinging, but he still felt weird.

As if there were an invisible glass shell around him or something.

He knew Matt expected him to come back with an insult, but he couldn't. "Ready to swim?" he challenged Matt. "I'll race you across the quarry pool."

"Lake," said Matt, pointing at the new sign above the park's entrance. "It's not a dumb old quarry pool anymore, it's Greenfield Lake, doofus."

The town had finally decided, since they couldn't stop kids from swimming at the old quarry, to turn the place into a park. Sand had been trucked in for a small beach. There were picnic tables and lifeguards.

The old stone-quarry pool was exactly the same. Only now it was called Greenfield Lake. Naturally everybody made fun of the grandiose name.

But Luke didn't answer. He was already racing for the water, shedding his T-shirt as he ran. He felt like he was trying to run away from himself.

At the first shock of the water, he felt like he had succeeded. In that instant, nothing existed but the icy clearness of the pool.

Luke surfaced, sputtering and hooting, and began to stroke for the opposite side, feeling good. He heard a sound, like a shriek. But it didn't register.

His skin tingled. His muscles felt strong working against the water. He could do this all day. Swim and swim and never have another thought.

He reached the far side of the pool, turned, and pushed off with his feet. Luke was feeling like himself again.

He ducked his head under the cold water and kicked, gliding like a missile under the surface. Down here everything was quiet and still. He made it almost all the way back across the pool before he had to come up for air.

"Good going, jock-brain." It was Matt, standing at the side, shaking his big head. "That was Mandy you splashed, diving in. She was on the ladder, dipping her toes. She looks ticked, man."

The quarry pool dropped off deep from limestone walls. There were only two ways into the water. Luke's way — a quick dive from the side. Or the new way — down the ladder the town had installed.

Luke remembered the shriek he had barely heard after he dived in. He felt like a total jerk. So much for any chance he might have had with Mandy.

"I never saw her," he protested. "I didn't know she was there."

"Yeah, well, that's not what she thinks," Matt said, smirking. "She thinks you did it on purpose. And then swam off without a word."

Luke's heart sank. "I'll have to go apologize." His stomach churned at the prospect.

Hauling himself up on the rock wall, his practiced foot found one of the many toeholds in the limestone. Matt leaped over Luke's head into the water, making a huge splash. Luke scarcely noticed.

His eyes were on Mandy. His stomach was churning worse than ever.

Mandy was talking to Sue Ellen. They were both laughing. No way he could go talk to

Mandy now. He wondered if they were laughing about what a geek he was. Luke shivered — and it wasn't from the coolness of the morning breeze on his wet skin.

Then his eye caught another movement at the park entrance. A large group of kids streaming in, mostly boys. A gang of skinheads, swaggering and rowdy.

Except for the one in front. The leader. Quentin.

Unlike his followers, Quentin hadn't shaved his head. His straggly dark hair hung straight to his shoulders. With those behind him dressed all in black, his bright orange swim trunks stood out like a beacon.

Quentin was skinny, his arms and legs like toothpicks. He had bad skin. He was short, too, and round-shouldered, and wore thick, heavy glasses. But he walked across the small beach like he owned it. Like he was six feet tall and as handsome as Brad Pitt.

He was striding purposefully toward Mandy.

Luke had felt a strange dread grip him the instant Quentin appeared.

Now a panicky urge came over him. He wanted to leap out of the pool and run to protect Mandy from Quentin. It was crazy. But the certainty of danger was so strong Luke didn't even question it.

He levered himself up on his arms. His

breath was fast and shallow. Then all at once the strength drained out of his arms like water out of a sieve.

Luke collapsed, chest down on the gritty edge of the pool. His legs dangled uselessly in the water. All of his strength was gone. All he could do was watch.

Mandy had her back to Quentin, but Luke could tell the instant she sensed him behind her. Mandy stiffened. Her face froze.

Sue Ellen kept chattering like she didn't notice a thing.

Quentin kept coming. The gang of 'heads fanned out behind him. They were going to surround Mandy, pen her in.

Luke's arms and legs felt made of rubber. He opened his mouth to yell a warning. No sound came out.

Instead a frightening image slammed into his brain. It blotted out the sun, the park.

Disoriented, Luke struggled to find himself. Panic gripped him, sending his head into a spin.

In his mind he saw himself pinned, unable to move. He didn't know where he was. But bending over him was Quentin.

He saw Quentin's muddy gray eyes gleaming with triumph. His rubbery mouth stretched wide in horrible glee. He said something. Luke couldn't hear any sound. But he could read Quentin's lips.

"Gotcha."

A spike of terror pierced him, and then suddenly the image vanished.

The sun was shining again. The pool sparkled all around him.

Luke saw Quentin reach Mandy on the beach. Although Quentin was a long distance away, Luke could tell he was wearing that same horrible grin that had invaded his mind.

Quentin extended a hand to grab Mandy's shoulder. An instant before he touched her, she whirled.

Luke felt strength flow back into his muscles. He gripped the stone under him.

But as he tensed to heave himself out of the water, a powerful force grabbed his foot and yanked him backwards into the pool.

The last thing he saw was the look of terror on Mandy's face.

Then the icy water closed over his head.

Chapter Six

Mandy felt a prickle between her shoulder blades, like an ice cube melting down her spine.

"There's Quentin," said Sue Ellen, perking up, straightening her shoulders. "There's something about him lately, have you noticed?"

Mandy had been feeling sluggish and out of it all morning. It was a struggle just to talk. Now the dark blot that had lurked in her brain since she woke up began to spread, like spilled ink.

"Mostly it's his skin, I guess," said Sue Ellen, tossing her head so her short brown curls bounced. "I told my little sister she should ask Quentin what kind of zit cream he's using. It's done wonders. He's almost good-looking now."

Mandy shuddered at the very thought of Quentin. Her throat closed up. She couldn't speak.

But Sue Ellen didn't notice. She was smiling flirtatiously over Mandy's shoulder.

"Ooh, he's coming this way." Sue Ellen cocked a hip and let her short terry cover-up fall open, showing off her Day-Glo yellow bikini. "I swear, he's making me feel tingly. But it's you he's looking at."

Darkness flooded Mandy's brain. She wanted to run like a scared little girl. But that was ridiculous.

Quentin was nobody. Nothing. An insignificant creep. She struggled to find her voice.

"How can you talk like that, Sue Ellen? He's revolting," Mandy said vehemently, her voice hoarse. "What about your puppy? Have you forgotten about that?"

Last year there had been a rash of small animal disappearances. Sue Ellen's new puppy, Smokey, had been one of the missing animals. She had put up posters all over town, but no one had seen the little dog.

Then one day Quentin had ridden his bicycle to school. Dangling like trophies from the handlebars were two furry tails. One looked like a squirrel tail. The other looked exactly like Smokey's tail.

Sue Ellen had been hysterical, but of course no one could prove anything. It was just a little brown tail, and Quentin said he had bought it at a yard sale, cheap.

Mandy would never forget the gloating pleasure Quentin had taken in Sue Ellen's distress. As if he fed hungrily on her grief.

A few days later, when her bouts of sobbing had diminished, the tail had shown up in a little coil in her school locker. Quentin had sworn that someone stole it off his bike.

But Mandy had seen how Sue Ellen's tears energized him.

Now Sue Ellen shook her head regretfully. "Quentin would never do a thing like that. It was just that he was so yucky-looking. We blamed him for everything. It was really mean of us, Mandy. You should try to be more tolerant."

Sue Ellen lifted her hand in a flirty little wave.

Mandy felt sick. And then suddenly there was a sharp pain in her back, near her right shoulder.

She felt a bolt of fear go through her like a jolt of electricity. It rooted her to the spot.

In her mind she saw a fist raised. In the fist was a long sharp needle, glinting in the sun. It was poised to plunge into her back.

Then a face filled her mind, a laughing, grinning horror of a face. Right out of last night's nightmare.

"Quentin!" Mandy shrieked, whirling suddenly, heart pounding.

There was no vicious-looking needle. But the face was there, in the flesh.

Quentin grinned at her, savoring her fear. His eyes bored into hers. The same eyes she'd seen in her nightmare.

Mandy couldn't look away. She knew he could see everything she was feeling. She also knew that such a power was impossible, ridiculous.

Her skin crawled with loathing.

"Lookin' good, Mandy," Quentin said, running his slimy tongue slowly over his bottom lip. "Amazing what a night without sleep can do for a girl."

Another jolt of anxiety electrified Mandy. How did Quentin know?

Strange pictures flashed in her head. Quentin's face looming close to hers. Behind him, large, glittering insect eyes. Watching. Observing.

She had a ghostlike memory of strange instruments prodding her flesh. She smelled a heavy, fetid odor.

The images flickered and vanished so quickly Mandy couldn't focus on any of them. Her heart was racing. She clenched her fists to try and stop her trembling.

Quentin stepped closer to her. His eyes slid over her hungrily.

She felt his gaze shred her oversize T-shirt. Rip through the thin one-piece bathing suit she was wearing underneath.

The naked feeling was so real she was startled to look down and see her clothing intact.

Quentin laughed, a low, growly sound, thick with mucus. His gaze lingered on her body, loving her distress.

He moved even closer. "You're mine now, Mandy girl," he whispered in her ear. "Mine in ways you can't even begin to imagine."

Mandy could hardly breathe.

She knew, with every fiber of her being, that if she didn't get away from Quentin now, his words would come true.

She stumbled backwards.

Her legs were shaky. Her body felt awkward.

Mirth dancing in his cold eyes, Quentin reached out a hand to steady her.

Mandy snatched her arm away in panic. She could not, *would not*, let him touch her.

"Stay away from me," she croaked hoarsely. The sound of her own voice trickled strength back into her body. She straightened. "Just keep away from me, you creep."

She heard Sue Ellen gasp in surprise. Mandy snatched up her day pack.

As she turned her back on Quentin, Mandy was startled to see seven or eight skinhead kids ranged in a loose, half-menacing circle around her, like an uncertain pack of wolves.

Quentin had so dominated her attention, she hadn't even been aware of their presence.

His cool, mocking voice hit her between the shoulder blades. "That's so cute, Mandy. So sweet."

He paused, and his oily laugh rang out low and slow. "And so very, very lame."

One of the skinhead entourage moved in front of her, blocking her path. He had a lightning bolt tattooed on the side of his face, and the cheap silver ring in his nose flashed in the sun.

But Mandy was beyond being intimidated by some wanna-be outlaw who was at least a grade behind her in school. Anger flared in her eyes. She strode past the skinhead, shouldering him aside with her pack.

Quentin's laughter followed her like a deadly gas. It rang in her ears and swirled around her head, fogging her vision.

She felt the mocking noise cling to her like mist, sapping her strength.

Her steps slowed. It was a struggle to place one foot in front of the other.

Quentin was winning. Somehow he was exerting control over her.

Mandy's legs shook. She knew if she fell now, Quentin would be all over her. A small cry escaped her as she pictured Quentin's moist limbs covering her, embracing her. The image was so real.

As if it had already happened.

Mandy shuddered so hard she stumbled onto one knee. Instantly, she felt Quentin's noxious breath on her neck.

Soft, evil laughter filled her ears like viscous oil.

Mandy's vision dimmed as horror overtook her.

Chapter Seven

Luke gulped reflexively as the frigid water closed over his head. He sputtered and struggled for the surface. But something big had him by the ankle.

It tugged him deeper.

Icy liquid flowed down his throat. His heart slammed against his ribs. His lungs burned for air. Up above he could see the bright shimmering surface.

He was drowning.

Luke kicked, hard. His foot sank into something clammy and soft. The hold on his ankle let go.

He clawed the water and kicked for the surface, but it was so far away. Luke felt himself sinking. He'd swallowed too much water.

Suddenly something big slammed into Luke from behind.

Panic burst in his brain. He opened his mouth to scream. Almost instantly he realized what he had done, but it was too late. Water rushed down his throat, choking him.

Luke began to black out. The water felt warmer. He was hardly aware of the creature pulling at him.

Then an image filled his mind. Quentin again, with that horrible gloating grin. Luke, pinned and helpless before him. But this time Luke saw more figures behind Quentin.

The figures he saw were humanoid but not human. Their faces were deathly pale. They had narrow chins and wide bulging foreheads.

But strangest of all were their huge, glittering eyes. They were round and multifaceted, like insect eyes. There was no white at all. Just that glittery iridescent blackness.

One loomed closer over Quentin's shoulder. Luke could see there was no feeling at all in the eyes, just a cold, calculating intelligence.

A movement caught his attention. The thing's arm was coming into his constricted view. It was holding an instrument. A silver-tipped point was aimed right at Luke's eye.

There was something weird about the arm. But Luke was too terrified to see what it was. He struggled against his bonds.

And then suddenly the image vanished.

Luke was back in the real world. He was coughing and heaving water. His lungs ached and his throat burned. Someone was holding him up.

"Wow, man, what happened?" It was Matt.

He pulled Luke to the ladder, stroking through the water with one arm while he held Luke up with the other. "I thought you were going to drown. You scared me good, man."

Luke felt sluggish. He was having trouble piecing together what had happened. All he knew for sure was he had experienced another of those blackout episodes.

His grandmother used to call them turns. "It's nothing," she'd say. "Just a bad turn." In the end, the "turns" had killed her.

Luke grabbed hold of the ladder and pushed Matt away irritably. "You grabbed my foot and pulled me in, didn't you, you jerk?"

"Hey, it was a joke," Matt protested, color returning to his white face now that Luke was talking again. "You've done it to me enough times."

Suddenly Luke remembered Mandy. He gasped and scrambled up the ladder.

But Mandy was gone. Luke couldn't see her anywhere.

Had she gotten away?

"Luke, what are you doing? What's going on?" Matt yelled after him.

"It's okay," Luke called back to his friend. "I've got to go."

He scanned the beach again. No Mandy.

But he spotted the skinheads. They were lounging around a picnic table in the grassy area.

Luke headed toward them. The skinheads turned to stare at him. As they shifted, Luke saw Quentin. He was sitting on the edge of the table, his skinny legs dangling.

He had some kind of shiny object in his hands.

When he got close, Luke could see Mandy wasn't with them. He let out his breath in relief and felt his chest loosen, surprised to realize how tense he'd been.

And how relieved he was now that he wouldn't have to speak to Quentin.

Luke started to turn back. Then the sun glinted off the thing in Quentin's hands. It looked strange, but somehow familiar. Was it a knife?

His heart began a dull thudding beat. Luke stopped.

Like a sleepwalker, Luke began moving unwillingly toward Quentin once more. He felt as if he were being drawn on a tether. His eyes were glued to the glinting thing in Quentin's hands.

The sun flashed again as Quentin tossed the silvery object from hand to hand. It was too long and thin to be a knife.

Fear pooled in Luke's chest. His breathing grew constricted. But his feet kept moving. He didn't stop until he could see the cold amusement in Quentin's eyes, magnified behind the thick lenses.

"What —" Luke tried to speak, but his throat had gone dry. All that came out was a croak. He swallowed as the skinhead crowd laughed, a little too loud and a little too long.

Something about their laughter tugged at the back of his mind. Luke ignored it, his eyes glued to the silvery object.

Quentin was tossing the thing between his hands so fast that it was only a blur. Try as he might, Luke couldn't focus on it.

"What is that?" he asked, forcing out the words.

Quentin only smiled, stretching his lips into a thin, sneering line. The thing jumped even more quickly between his hands. Could human hands move that fast?

"What's it to you, anyway?" jeered one of the skinheads.

The familiar voice snagged Luke's attention. His head jerked up and he was looking into his brother's face. That's what had bothered him about the laughter. Some of it was Jeff's.

His chest felt hollow with dismay. What was Jeff mixed up in? Luke had to try and get him out of here. "What are you doing with this guy?"

Jeff rolled his eyes. "Oh, puleeeze. Don't give me that big brother routine."

"Jeff, look, whatever Quentin is up to, you don't want to be part of it." Luke knew it was useless. He could feel his words rippling through the other kids, stirring them to laughter. He was only making things worse.

Then Jeff stepped closer, out of the shadows, and Luke got another shock. What he had thought was a smear of dirt was a tattoo. A jagged lightning bolt stretched from brow to chin.

Luke was speechless.

Jeff opened his mouth to speak. Quentin held up a hand. Luke's brother snapped his jaws shut again, obeying an unspoken command. Luke's attention snapped back to Quentin.

The silvery thing was gone from sight. Quentin was plainly displeased — Jeff's interruption had disrupted the focus of whatever dumb mind game he was playing.

"You still don't get it, Luke," Quentin said. "It's you who don't want to be part of 'it.' And for you, it's too late. Way too late."

Quentin's calm, contemptuous tone sliced through Luke. He felt a sharp pain in his chest. His blood froze in his veins.

He had to get out of there. Now.

But he couldn't move.

Quentin hopped off the table and started toward him. The sun bounced off his glasses, hiding his eyes.

But Luke didn't need to see their expression. Quentin's lips twitched in a cruel smile.

Luke knew the pain would be real this time.

Chapter Eight

Mandy didn't stop running until her lungs burned and her legs gave out. She was startled to realize she was in front of the library, some three miles from the park.

She sank down on the low concrete wall out front, chest heaving, heart slamming.

What an idiot she must have looked, racing through town as if the devil himself were after her.

Well, that's the way she had felt.

But it made no sense. What had frightened her so badly? Laughter from a gang of jeering boys? The revolting threats and insinuations of a sociopathic geek?

Quentin was lower on the evolutionary scale than the average worm. Why had she felt so frightened? And worse, so powerless?

Mandy sank her head in her hands, fighting

off tears. She felt as if there was a dark place inside herself that she couldn't reach. It was eating at her, taking chunks from her sanity.

Sitting there, the scene in the quarry park replayed in her mind like a nightmare belonging to someone else.

She remembered sinking to her knees, the terror of Quentin's laughter, how powerless she had felt to escape.

It had taken a tremendous effort of will to raise her head and fix her gaze on the park entrance. She had pushed herself to her feet. Walling off her mind, she focused completely on getting out of the park as if her *life* depended on it.

Mandy had felt if she could only reach the road, she'd be safe. But safe from what?

And then when she finally reached the street, she had stopped only long enough to pull her shorts on over her damp bathing suit. Immediately she had begun to run like she'd never run before.

As if speed could outdistance the images in her own head.

First last night's weird blackout and then today's even weirder encounter. She shuddered again, remembering how exposed and vulnerable she had felt when Quentin ran his eyes over her body.

She had felt as if he'd known about last night.

As if he'd *been* there, somehow, inside her mind.

But that was nuts. Quentin was the same nasty little vermin he'd always been, nothing more. He had always creeped her out, for as long as she could remember.

Some of it was his looks, she had to admit. Quentin looked like a rat.

He had pointy little features with sharp beady eyes and sharp little teeth sticking out over his bottom lip. He was short and skinny and twitchy. His ratty hair was greasy and lank. He was a geek with a face like a cratered moon of pus-filled volcanoes.

Maybe Sue Ellen was right, and his skin was improving. Mandy hadn't noticed. But nothing would improve his personality because Quentin liked himself the way he was.

That was what made her skin crawl. It wasn't just his creepy looks. There was a sneaky, nasty, secretive aura about him, and lately it was worse, more menacing.

Quentin took pleasure in other people's humiliation and pain. He had no friends, not real friends, but you couldn't feel sorry for him. He wanted it that way. Mandy had always had the feeling Quentin didn't regard other people as quite real. For him, human beings were objects of amusement.

With a jolt of unease, Mandy realized she'd

never seen him with the skinhead gang before today. And yet suddenly he was their leader. But how? What did it mean?

Mandy shook her head in frustration. Why was she wasting so much time thinking about Quentin? Yes, he had upset her, even frightened her. But he was just a symptom.

There was something seriously wrong with her, and she had to find out what it was. Maybe it was just some weird combination of nightmares, sleepwalking, and lack of sleep.

But it could be something serious. She had heard that mental illness often struck in the teen years. She could be psycho. Or maybe it was a hormone imbalance, something simple like that.

Mandy looked up at the ugly library building. Her unconscious must have directed her here. While she'd been fleeing like a scared rabbit, her brain had still been working for her.

She got up off the wall and walked toward the library with her usual twinge of distaste. The library was in an old factory. It was a grimy brick building with small windows. Inside, it was always dark and chilly, even on sunny, warm days. Not a cozy place.

Hurrying up the library steps, she pulled open the heavy door, going in before her reluctance could get the better of her.

She stopped inside the door to let her eyes adjust. The lighting was dim after the brilliant sunshine outside. And the air smelled musty. The building was oppressively silent. It had to be the least inviting library in the world. Even though she loved to read, she always dreaded coming to this place.

"Oh!" Mandy started as she spied a figure staring at her through the gloom. "Mrs. Grundy. I didn't see you."

The sour-faced librarian grunted in reply and moved behind the massive central desk. Mrs. Grundy had been librarian as long as Mandy could remember. She always acted as if she didn't much like anyone using the library, and she especially disliked children and teenagers.

Mandy ducked her head and scurried across the lobby to the stairs. She went up, feeling the old lady's bad-tempered eyes on her. The old wooden stairs creaked. The sound seemed to rip rudely through the silence. Mandy winced, feeling herself beginning to sweat nervously.

She was uncomfortably aware that there was no one in the building but her and Mrs. Grundy.

On the second floor, Mandy went straight to the computerized catalogue. In moments, she had found just what she needed and headed for the stacks. The medical section was at the far end.

Slipping down the narrow aisle between the tall stacks, Mandy instantly felt hemmed in. But the book was right where it was supposed to be. She grabbed it and sneezed as a spray of dust was dislodged. No one had touched this book in a long time.

Just as she sat down at a secluded corner table and opened the book, a sound made her freeze. A creak on the stairs.

Mandy listened for footsteps, the hair rising on the back of her neck. Nothing. She pictured Mrs. Grundy standing halfway up the stairs, spying.

Mandy whirled. Her chair scraped the floor loudly. There was no one there.

She turned back to the book, disgusted with herself. She'd never been the jumpy, imaginative type. She hated what was happening to her.

The Encyclopedia of Brain Diseases. The heavy book's title seemed to leap off the cover. Mandy swallowed. She felt so lost and alone.

In the table of contents she found a chapter on "Fugue States: Blackouts and Memory Loss." Feeling a little queasy, she opened to the page and began reading.

Her shoulders slumped as she read. Her eyes followed the small print with growing horror. Her symptoms were described in every detail. And the possible causes were horrible.

Brain tumor. Stroke. Epilepsy.

The stairs creaked. Mandy stiffened, instantly alert. The boards creaked again, a loud protest. And this time she heard footsteps.

They were too heavy to be Mrs. Grundy's.

And then they stopped. He — whoever it was — was up here with her. Mandy sat rigid in her chair, listening intently. She heard nothing. Was he watching her?

Then after a few minutes, the footsteps started again. The person was moving toward her. But he was being very quiet, moving very slowly, as if he was trying to sneak up on her.

Mandy's pulse quickened. If she screamed, there was no one to hear except Mrs. Grundy.

Sliding, almost silent, the steps crept closer.

She remembered the dust she'd raised, getting her book. There was nothing at this end of the library anyone was interested in. Nothing but her.

She fought the urge to flee. She was being ridiculous, she knew she was. This was the public library. What could happen to her here?

Suddenly an image burst in her brain like a clenched fist.

Quentin's leering, lip-smacking face gloating over her.

His footsteps. Coming to get her.

Chapter Nine

Quentin came closer, closer.

The smile got wider. Yellow teeth clicked together eagerly.

Little yips of glee escaped him.

Quentin's face filled Luke's vision. And still it moved closer until his flashing glasses, flaring nostrils, and yellow grin were one big blur.

"Boo!"

The sound popped in Luke's ears. Spittle spattered his face. His muscles jerked. He could move again.

Luke turned clumsily and stumbled.

Quentin's cackling laughter rang out.

Luke heard Jeff's laughter joining in as he struggled to find his footing, his legs rubbery.

"Should we stop him for ya, Q?" another boy asked.

"No. Let him go. I'll let him squirm on the hook a little longer." Quentin slapped his knee as he hooted with glee.

The sound rang in Luke's ears long after the boys had lost interest in him. Anger replaced his fear, but he felt helpless to do anything about it.

Luke scooped his T-shirt up off the sand, slapping it against his leg as he headed out of the park. But as his anger faded, a hollow feeling replaced it. He had never felt so alone.

No one could help him with what was happening. No one but himself. He trudged up the street, too drained to run.

Luke picked up the pace as he went through town. He waved to a few people he knew, but didn't stop like he normally would. He didn't stop until he reached the public library.

The squat ugly building had always made him feel small and inadequate. Although, Luke thought as he pushed through the door, it wasn't the building that bothered him so much as its guardian.

That old bag Mrs. Grundy. She always glared at him like she expected him to start smuggling books out under his shirt.

She glared now as Luke faked a smile and headed swiftly upstairs. The air in the building had a thickness and weight to it. Luke wanted to start whistling to liven the atmosphere, but that might give the old bat a heart attack.

Instead he found himself treading lightly, trying to make as little noise as possible. In the card catalogue he found several books that might help.

Then, on second thought, he turned back to the catalogue. There was a good possibility, a very good possibility, he had to admit, that what was wrong with him was medical.

The way he was thinking — his paranoia — was probably a symptom. He could have some rare brain fever that caused blackouts and totally mind-bending hallucinations.

The Encyclopedia of Brain Diseases. That was certainly clear enough. He'd get that one first, then look for the others. Luke moved slowly down the stacks, checking the numbers. The medical books seemed to be all the way at the end.

As he entered the last stack, a chair scraped. Startled, Luke jumped. He'd thought he was alone.

A familiar figure hurried past the stack in a blur. Her blond hair swung forward, hiding her face. But there was no way he could mistake those long, slim legs.

Mandy Durgin.

What was she doing in the library on a day

like this? He knew she was a brain but, still, it was summer. Too bad she hadn't seen him in the library. It might have scored him some points.

Luke ran his eye down the spines of the books, trying to put Mandy out of his mind.

She seemed nice and she sure was great-looking. But she hung with a totally different crowd. Astronomy club. Tie-dyed clothes and the vegetarian plate for lunch. New Age hippie types.

Besides, he didn't have room in his life for girls right now. He had to find out what was happening to him before he ended up in the loony bin. Or worse.

The medical book wasn't on the shelf. Luke gave up looking. He found his other books easily enough. He was kind of dreading the ordeal of checking them out with Mrs. Grundy. She was sure to have some sarcastic remark.

But when he came downstairs, Mrs. Grundy wasn't at the front desk. Mandy was. Luke squared his shoulders. He hoped there weren't any sweat stains on his T-shirt. At least he wasn't sweating now. This place was cold as a tomb.

Mandy looked over her shoulder, a frightened look on her face. When she saw who it was, she tried to smile. But her face was stiff.

What did Mandy have to be afraid of?

She was holding some big thick book. The front was pressed to her chest so he couldn't see the title.

"I don't know where Mrs. Grundy went," Mandy said nervously as Luke stopped beside her. "I've been waiting five minutes at least."

"We're the only ones in here," said Luke. "You'd think she might notice we want to check out books. Old witch," he added under his breath.

Mandy stifled a giggle.

The sound made Luke brave. "I know how we can get her attention," he said. "We'll start to leave with the books. She'll notice us then."

Mandy smiled. It looked almost real this time. "She'd probably have us arrested. Dragged off in chains. I'll bet she's hiding somewhere back there," Mandy said, indicating the shadowy recesses of the library. "Watching."

"Mrs. Grundy!" Luke called loudly, surprising even himself. Was there anything he wouldn't do to impress this girl?

But Mandy's eyes widened in what looked like admiration, so he tried again. "Hey, Grundy!"

A door slammed somewhere. Brisk footsteps headed their way. Luke's insides quailed as Mrs. Grundy's scowling face came into view.

But he stood straight and gave her a big

smile. "We thought maybe you'd gone to lunch," he said. "Forgot we were here."

The librarian didn't reply. She marched behind the desk and fixed a fierce, thin-lipped glare on him. She held out her hand for his books.

"Mandy was here first," said Luke, a little breathlessly. It was bad enough Mrs. Grundy would have to see them. He really didn't want Mandy to know what books he was taking out.

"No, you go ahead. Please," Mandy insisted.

Luke had no choice. He pushed the books across the desk surface, heat rising to his face in a fierce blush.

He turned toward Mandy, trying to block her view of the titles. "So how's your summer going so far?" he asked cheerfully.

He should have known he wouldn't get off that easy.

"*Aliens Among Us?*" Mrs. Grundy's grating voice boomed out in disbelief. "*Alien Abductees: In Their Own Words?* You pull me away from my work for this trash?" Mrs. Grundy snorted, stamped the books hard, and shoved them back at Luke.

Luke felt his face flaming. He would have bolted out the door, but he didn't want to leave Mandy to deal with the old bat alone.

"Well?" rasped the librarian impatiently, her bony fingers tapping.

Mandy was still clutching her book. Reluctantly, she put it down.

Luke gasped. "Hey, I was looking for that," he said without thinking.

Mrs. Grundy's head snapped back toward him. "What are *you* waiting for? This is a library, you know, not a dating service. You've created quite enough commotion in here."

Luke backed off. He moved in a trance for the exit. Pushed open the door. Went out.

His thoughts were whirling. Two people in the library at the same time on a gorgeous day, both looking for *The Encyclopedia of Brain Diseases.*

It couldn't be a coincidence.

But what else could it be?

He looked at his own books. Was he really so far gone that he would take a coincidence like this for proof? No.

But as he saw Mandy heading toward him, Luke decided to take a huge chance. Here he was, a guy who never asked a girl on a date unless he was absolutely, positively certain she would say yes. And now he was about to tell a virtual stranger — a girl — what had happened to him last night.

Luke opened the door for Mandy. "Say," he said with forced heartiness. "You, um, want to go to The Upside for a cappuccino or something?"

Mandy looked surprised. "Oh. I . . . I —"

He was about to get shot down. He felt his face get hot again.

"You kids!" Mrs. Grundy's shrill voice penetrated the heavy glass doors. "No loitering!"

Mandy's soft blue eyes suddenly got steely. She flashed a look back through the door. "Why doesn't she get on her broomstick and go back where she came from," Mandy snapped.

"Oz won't have her," Luke replied. "They got rid of her and they're not taking her back."

Mandy laughed and thought for a moment. "I'd love a coffee," she said.

He smiled in relief and they fell into step, heading back downtown.

And then suddenly they seemed to run out of things to say.

Luke was wondering how to begin. Nothing seemed quite right.

"Sorry I'm not such great company," Mandy said suddenly. "I didn't sleep too well last night."

"Me, neither," said Luke, his heart beginning to thump. This was his opening. "That's why I was in the library, looking for that book you took out."

Mandy's reaction stunned him. Her face drained of color. Her blue eyes stood out against her white skin, like sapphires on snow. Her eyes held his. A current seemed to flow between them.

"What do you mean?" she asked, almost whispering.

Luke's voice faltered at first. It was taking him a long time to get to the point, but Mandy didn't hurry him. She just nodded and let him know she was listening.

"The high-tension wires started sputtering at the junction — the place where the big poles cross at the top of the hill."

"I know where the junction is," said Mandy. "My dad is an engineer with the power company."

"The lines were sparking and crackling, and when I looked up it was like something big was swallowing up the sky — the stars, moon, everything disappeared," Luke said, his voice cracking as he remembered.

"The next thing I knew I was in my room, in bed, fully dressed. It was two A.M. and my parents were having fits downstairs wondering where I was."

Mandy's face was hidden behind that smooth curtain of hair. "Have you had any residual effects? Paranoia, hallucinations, things like that?"

"Yeah," Luke answered eagerly. "You, too?"

Mandy's eyes narrowed a fraction. "How did you know?"

Luke was brought up short. It was just a feeling he had. How could he explain it?

"There were a lot of clues," he said, shrugging. "Both of us being in the library looking for that book, you saying you didn't sleep last night, the —"

He stopped. He'd been about to mention the scene on the beach. Quentin, the aura of danger he'd sensed around her. But something told him Mandy wouldn't be able to absorb so much at once.

She was looking at him quizzically. "The what?" she asked.

Luke tried to smile. "I don't know. The expression on your face, I guess. Scared and worried. Like mine."

She nodded back at him. "Well, you're right. I did have a similar experience. Only I started out in my room at ten o'clock and came to on my porch at two A.M. I figured it was some weird sleepwalking thing, only my brain has been, uh, jumpy ever since. But your description gave me an idea. I think I know what happened."

Her intense expression energized Luke. Could this really be something normal? Something explainable?

"It's the high-tension lines that made me think of it. My dad has been complaining about a series of power surges lately. You were under the high-tension junction and I only live three blocks from there," Mandy explained. She stopped on the sidewalk and faced him with an air of total confidence. "I think it was a huge electrical surge that affected us both, made us blank out. I'll bet there are others who were nearby who had the same experience."

"But it didn't affect your parents," Luke said, unconvinced. "They were right there."

Mandy waved off his objection. "It makes sense that kids our age would be most susceptible. During the adolescent years there's a lot of electrical activity in the brain. Some of it seems random and, of course, some teens throw off more energy than others. You've heard of poltergeists?"

"Sure," said Luke. He didn't think he was the poltergeist type. But Mandy was forging ahead, as if quoting out of one of the books she'd been reading. This was the Mandy he remembered from class, brainy beyond belief. Way too smart for an average guy like him.

"The surge must have been in synch with the energy being generated by our own brains," said Mandy. "Causing some sort of overload."

Mandy gripped his arm. The touch of her fingers sent a surge of its own through Luke.

"Come on," she said. "Hurry. I'll bet we find three or four more kids who had similar experiences. Kids who live near that junction. Maybe one or two of them will be at The Upside."

Luke looked toward the cafe. It was just up the street. He wasn't sure it was good idea for Mandy to burst in, asking for blackout sufferers.

"I don't know," Luke said doubtfully. "Electrical energy doesn't explain how I somehow got past my parents into my bedroom."

Mandy frowned impatiently. "There must be some way you could sneak past your parents if you really wanted to. A back door? A tree by your window? The surge overrode your consciousness but not your cunning," Mandy suggested.

Luke could picture it, barely. He could have sneaked in the back door, waited until his parents left the living room, and scooted up the stairs. It wouldn't have been easy, but it was possible.

He nodded cautiously. "And the afterimages — those would be like the sparks off the wire, extra energy firing off hallucinations in the brain?"

"Right," said Mandy.

Luke noticed her shudder slightly and knew her "hallucinations" were as unpleasant as his. Did her visions also involve Quentin?

Luke was certain they did. He was less certain that they were experiencing hallucinations.

The cafe door swung open and a group of kids spilled out onto the sidewalk. Luke tensed.

It was Quentin, along with Jeff and some of the other skinhead followers.

But Mandy hadn't noticed. "Naturally there's some electrical residue left over," she went on, intent on her explanation. "It's working itself out, sparking unexpectedly. It's unpleasant, so the brain interprets it unpleasantly, like nightmares. At least that's the way mine have been." She looked up at him. "Yours, too?"

But Luke had stopped listening. He'd gone as rigid as a statue.

Another nightmare vision had invaded his brain. But this time he wasn't the focus.

Mandy was.

Chapter Ten

"Luke?" A spike of alarm went through Mandy. Luke had stopped, his eyes fixed and unseeing.

She reached to tug his arm and pulled back her hand with a cry of shock. His arm was as hard and cold as stone. "Luke? What's wrong?"

A bray of laughter snapped her head around.

Quentin was standing on the sidewalk, looking at them. The sun flashed off his glasses, straight into her eyes. Mandy blinked and flinched away.

"It's so nice to see you, Mandy," Quentin said. His tone made "nice" sound like a dirty word. "But what are you doing with that meat brain? Brawn is cute, but its use is limited. Don't you agree?"

Mandy stepped in front of Luke as if to shield him. Her insides were quivering. She told herself not to be weak.

Quentin was between them and the cafe entrance. For such a scrawny creep, he seemed to take up a lot of room. Mandy slid her hand behind her back and poked Luke. No response.

"He's not quite ready to resume his limited existence yet, Mandy my love," Quentin purred. "He's learning his place in the scheme of things."

"Get out of our way," Mandy demanded. She wished her voice had more force.

Quentin threw back his head. His greasy hair hung in lank clumps. He surveyed the sky with satisfaction and sucked in a deep breath of air.

"Oh, this is soo much fun," he cried. "I wish I could prolong it forever."

He lowered his head and focused on her. The tip of his tongue protruded between his ratty teeth. He licked his lips slowly.

Mandy stepped back, right into Luke. His body didn't yield, but his arms came around her protectively.

Quentin didn't like that. He stepped forward, anger flashing in his colorless beady eyes.

"There's something on the bulletin board inside that should interest you," he hissed. "Both of you."

Quentin moved closer still, his lips almost brushing Mandy's ear. "You think you're above it all, Mandy," he whispered. "But you're nothing unless I say you are."

Mandy recoiled from his words and his fetid breath. Quentin was no longer looking at her. He flicked a hand over his shoulder and his obedient acolytes moved into formation behind him.

Luke still didn't move, his arms locked around Mandy like a gate. As Quentin passed, he reached out a hand so quickly Mandy didn't have time to duck. His clammy fingers brushed the back of her neck.

A sick shiver ran down her spine. She cried out in fury. Quentin's laughter floated back at her.

Suddenly she felt life flow back into Luke.

"What?" He jumped, embarrassed to find his arms clasped around her. "S-sorry, Mandy," he stuttered. "I had one of those vision things. Like I blacked out. It was awful." His voice was hoarse and his hands were shaky.

He peered at her intently. "You're okay?"

"Sure." Mandy ducked away from the intensity of his gaze.

She had liked the strong feel of his arms around her. But Quentin had rattled her so much she didn't know what she was feeling. She couldn't even think straight.

"Let's go inside," she said. "I think we both need to sit down."

She could still feel the sluglike trail of Quentin's fingers at the top of her spine. His touch had felt so intimate . . . and worse, familiar.

She would never, in her entire life, let Quentin touch her again.

"You sure you're all right?" Luke persisted. His voice was soft and tender. "Did you have one of those, uh, hallucinations, too?"

"No. Really." Mandy shook her head, letting her hair fall forward to hide her face. "It's just that talking to Quentin Creep always upsets me."

"Quentin? So he *was* here."

"Yes." Mandy felt a pang of dismay. She *knew* it wasn't Quentin who had frozen Luke — it was an electrical spasm, shorting out his brain, putting him into a fugue state, as the medical book had described. But it gave her chills to realize he hadn't even known Quentin was there.

As Luke opened the cafe door, Mandy glanced up the street. She couldn't see Quentin, but the skinhead with the lightning tattoo was looking back at her, grinning wolfishly.

Luke grunted. "That's my brother, Jeff," he said. "I knew he'd become a real jerk, but I didn't know until today that he'd sunk low enough to be hanging out with Quentin."

They went inside. The place was dim and

cool. There were only a few people at the tables. Mandy glanced at the back wall where the bulletin board was. Everything that was happening in town got tacked up there.

She could see there was a big new yellow poster, but she couldn't read it from where she was standing.

She wasn't ready to tell Luke what Quentin had said. Or to go back and read the poster for herself. Any message from Quentin was sure to be bad news.

"Cappuccino?" Luke asked.

"Double latte," Mandy told him.

While Luke went to get the coffee, Mandy greeted a few kids she knew. Two of them lived closer to the power junction than she did. She asked if they had felt anything strange last night.

"Strange?" Kari cocked her head. "Like what? An earthquake or something?"

"An electrical feeling in the air," Mandy said, "like before a storm."

But Mandy already knew the answer. Kari and Gordy both seemed too normal. And that walled-in feeling was back again. Mandy felt like she was inside an invisible capsule and everybody else was outside.

Funny. She hadn't felt that at all with Luke.

She saw him threading his way toward her through the crowd. He looked so solid. Cute, too, with his jaw set so seriously. Plus, he had those soulful eyes. . . .

He set the drinks down on an empty table near the front and Mandy slid into a seat. Luke smiled. "Quentin Creep. I like that. It suits him."

Mandy laughed. "I've always called him that. Ever since he fed my goldfish to the neighbor's cat and held my arms so I couldn't save it." Even now she shuddered slightly at the memory. "We were both six at the time. He hasn't changed a bit."

"Except for the worse, maybe," Luke said, his smile gone.

Mandy sipped at her coffee. "He's been hassling me lately. Just before the semester ended he joined the astronomy club. And ever since, he's been acting like there's some connection between us. It's horrible."

Luke looked worried. "What did he say when we were outside? While I was in my trance or whatever."

"Oh." Mandy grimaced. "He said we should check out the bulletin board."

Luke's gaze flew over her head. He got up so quickly his chair almost fell over.

Instantly Mandy felt irritated with him. She had been enjoying their quiet moment. Why did Luke have to spoil it?

But she rose and followed him back to the

bulletin board. She saw his back go rigid. A stab of alarm went through her. Was Luke having another one of those catatonic episodes?

Could the electrical surge have made him epileptic? She had read that epilepsy was sometimes caused by a blow to the head.

She hurried toward him. In her concern, she forgot about the poster. And then Luke turned to her.

He wasn't catatonic. She sagged with relief.

But his skin had gone dead white. His lips were pressed in a bloodless line.

Luke looked as if he'd seen something worse than a ghost.

Chapter Eleven

Luke gestured weakly at the bulletin board. He felt like he'd just been hit by a train. His brain was working in low gear.

Mandy looked at the bulletin board. She looked back at him. There was disbelief in her clear eyes. And something else. Anger?

He stared again at the bold black letters.

ARE THERE ALIENS IN OUR MIDST?

Under the headline, it said, ABDUCTEES INVITED!

Then there was a blurb. It was the usual hysterical nonsense. Normally he would be the first to make fun of it.

"Luke! Hello?" Mandy frowned and rolled her eyes. "You're not taking this seriously? You can't be. It's some sick joke of Quentin's. You're playing right into his hands."

"What's Quentin got to do with it?" Luke protested. "Besides, what difference does it make if it's a joke? Satisfying your curiosity doesn't make you a believer. Right?"

Mandy's eyes flashed. Luke couldn't understand why she was getting so uptight about this.

"You think you were abducted by aliens last night, don't you?" Mandy demanded. She flicked her hand at the books tucked under his arm. *"Aliens Among Us, Abductees in Their Own Words."* She shook her head in disgust. "I should have known when I saw those books."

"Mandy! Wait," Luke called as she spun away from him. "I'm not the one with the closed mind," he said, dogging her heels as she stalked out the cafe door.

"Ha!" Mandy made a strangled sound of disbelief.

"It's true," Luke said. "Look at the facts. I think you're probably right. All this has something to do with the electrical power surges connecting up with our overenergized brains. But still, Mandy. It's the only possibility you're willing to consider. What if you're wrong? What if we *have* been abducted by aliens?"

Mandy made another disbelieving sound and increased her pace.

"Come on," Luke insisted. "What do you have to lose? I don't know about you, but I'm finding this whole experience a total one-hundred-percent bummer. I'm willing to try absolutely anything to get back to normal."

"You go ahead and do what you have to do," Mandy said, tossing her head. "I'm going to go home and read up on power surges. There's a scientific explanation for what happened to us — and it doesn't involve aliens. Aliens don't exist!"

Luke dropped back and let her go. He didn't know what was making her so angry, but he was only making things worse arguing.

He could kick himself for checking those alien books out of the library. If not for that, Mandy might have been willing to listen.

Disgusted with himself, Luke turned on his heel and headed back to the library. He dumped the two books in the outside return slot.

"There," he said to himself, suddenly feeling at a loss. He was right back where he had started from. And he hadn't told Mandy about that last awful vision.

Not that she would have believed him. As the world around him had faded, Luke had pictured Mandy, strapped to some kind of table or stretcher.

In his mind's eye, he'd seen her surrounded by shadowy creatures. He couldn't focus on them. But one thing he could see. They were not human.

Luke pushed the awful scene from his mind. He hoped Mandy was right. If what was happening was an electrical storm of the mind, then it would probably end soon.

But if she was wrong, he didn't want to be caught waiting around doing nothing. Waiting passively for something to finish digesting his brain.

Luke turned purposefully toward Old High Street. He would go back up to the power-line junction. Maybe there was something there. Some evidence he could show Mandy. Maybe they could figure it out together.

If he could get her to talk to him again.

Reaching Old High Street, Luke turned automatically. The road was empty. The scrubby woods on each side gave the whole scene a desolate feel.

But Luke was preoccupied. Thinking about Mandy. The graceful way she moved. The little pucker between her brows when she concentrated.

Even when she was angry, she was still a knockout. Most people's faces scrunched up and looked ugly when they got mad. But, though he hadn't noticed so much at the time, Mandy's eyes just got a brighter shade of blue and her nostrils flared in a very delicate way.

But it wasn't only her looks. She really listened to people when they talked. He liked the way she looked into his eyes and considered his words in a serious way. Although she hadn't done that in the end.

Luke slapped his fist against his thigh. Maybe the picture he'd built up of Mandy was wishful thinking. Just because she was beautiful.

What if the real Mandy was the stuck-up, do-it-my-way-or-no-way girl who'd stalked away from him, nose in the air? Why shouldn't that be the real Mandy?

Kicking up a chunk of rotten asphalt from the old road, Luke put her out of his mind.

Coming to the bottom of the hill, the steady buzz of the wires overhead snagged his full attention. Luke looked up, reluctant to go on.

One step at a time, he forced himself up the small rise. The sky was sunny and cloudless. It was silly to think anything could swoop out of such a sky and grab him.

But his nerves jangled. The crackling noise was getting louder. There was nothing weird about that. Still, Luke couldn't shake the feeling that the wires were buzzing excitedly among themselves. Waiting for him to come within their reach.

"Don't be such an idiot," he told himself. Out loud.

His voice was instantly gobbled up by the storm of energy overhead.

He reached the top. Walking over to the immense aluminum poles, he forced himself to stay and look around. He touched the pole. His nerves seemed to vibrate in tune with the wires. He snatched his hand off the pole as if he'd been burned.

This was the spot where it had happened. Starting from here, he had lost four hours of his life. And scrambled his brain.

But the area told him nothing.

Luke took a deep breath, then another, trying to calm himself. He stepped away from the pole, off the asphalt. There was a weedy area where the woods had been cut back.

Walking into the scraggly brush, Luke examined the ground. He wasn't sure what to look for. But if he'd had his brain fried here, there should be some sign. A burned patch, something.

He tried to shut out the menacing sizzle of the wires so he could concentrate. Methodically, he moved forward, scanning.

Something burst out of the dry grass at his feet. Luke jumped. It flew at his face. He scrambled backwards and it flew past his shoulder.

A grasshopper. Luke's heart was pounding erratically.

This was pointless. There was nothing here. He should go.

Talk to Mandy, apologize, do it her way. The important thing was to stick together. No one else knew what they were going through.

But instead, Luke found himself moving forward. He'd just go as far as the edge of the woods. Then he'd turn back.

Luke startled another grasshopper. He was absurdly pleased with himself for not jumping out of his skin again. Reaching the trees, he was about to turn back when a flash of brightness caught his eye.

He looked toward the spot, just a few feet into the woods. Nothing. He moved his head from side to side, slowly. There! Something shiny, reflecting in the sun.

It was probably a piece of broken glass. Luke's heart began to thud again, telling him to forget it, give up, go home. He moved cautiously toward the spot.

As if the shiny thing might fly up and bite him.

He was looking right at the spot, but he couldn't see the cause of the flash. He cocked his head, moved it from side to side, but whatever it was had disappeared.

That's impossible, Luke thought. He crouched down and began to run his hand over the leaf litter on the ground. "It was right here," he muttered to himself.

His fingers encountered something hard and

smooth. But he couldn't see what he was touching. His eyes were telling him there was nothing there. The hair stood up on the back of his neck.

Luke wanted to snatch his fingers away. Sweat was trickling down his spine. But he forced himself to run his fingers over the object, looking for an edge.

He found a jagged break. The edge was sharp, but not enough to cut him. Carefully, he scoped out its size. It was stuck to the dead leaves in a couple places, and was no bigger than his palm.

Only when he had peeled it free of the debris could Luke actually see it. And then only because bits of earth and leaf stuck to it.

It was as hard and clear as glass, but thin and as flexible as plastic.

Luke stood slowly, examining the almost invisible sheet. It was strange, but it certainly didn't look like an alien artifact. Just a scrap of something. He figured he'd show it to Mandy anyway.

Her father was an electrical engineer. Maybe he would know what it was.

As Luke turned to leave, something spiked between his shoulder blades, like a needle jab.

His heart instantly ratcheted up to piston speed. He felt eyes drilling him. And they weren't friendly.

Luke whirled, hoping to catch a sudden movement. The weedy waste ground looked undisturbed. He was alone. Except Luke somehow knew he was *not* alone.

His hand closed over his new find. Maybe he could still hide it. He slowly moved his hand toward his back pocket.

Suddenly there was a sharp flash. His hand stung. Luke cried out, blinded. Yellow spots burst red before his eyes.

He twisted toward where he thought the flash had come from. Was that a movement in the trees? Luke blinked, trying to clear his eyes of the bursting color spots.

There was a disturbance among the trees, leaves rustling. Luke saw a shimmer in the air. There *was* something there. But he couldn't quite make it out.

Eyes clearing, he looked down at his hand. The palm was blistered. There was nothing in his hand but a small pile of fine grains like ground sand.

A surge of anger overwhelmed his fear. He slid the grains into his pocket and started into the woods. He was going to track down whatever it was he'd seen in the trees.

Nobody was going to shoot things at him and get away with it.

Luke wound and pushed his way through the

trees and undergrowth. Leaves rustled ahead of him. He was close.

Luke's blood raced with adrenaline. His eyes scanned the woods intently. There! Another weird shimmer. As if he could actually see the air being displaced, rather than the thing displacing it.

Squinting, Luke focused hard on the fluttering tree leaves. He caught an outline, the motion of an arm, the lift of a running foot. But still the person — or thing — evaded his sight.

How could that be?

A trickle of cold fear ran with the sweat down his spine. But Luke kept his focus on the thing ahead of him.

It flitted between the trees and made a lot less noise than he did. But Luke was gaining on it. And his eyes were getting more practiced at seeing it.

His skin began to crawl. His sweat turned cold. He'd seen this creature before.

In his head.

The thing faltered. Luke thought he might have seen it stumble. It was tiring. Luke was catching up.

Part of his brain screamed at him to catch it. Nothing else mattered. Another part of his brain shrieked at him to turn around and run as fast as he could out of there.

Before it was too late.

If Luke had turned back he would have seen another creature step out of the trees behind him.

But Luke kept going, intent on his quarry.

The second creature's arm blurred as it was raised. Leveled, it settled into solidity again. Extended from the arm was a long silver instrument.

It was pointed deliberately and with care at the back of Luke's bobbing head. The silver point homed in precisely.

It flashed fire.

With a soft grunt, Luke fell.

Chapter Twelve

Everything was such a tremendous effort. Mandy forked up a bite of spinach lasagna that seemed to weigh a ton.

Her attempts to learn something from her father's technical manuals had been a bust. It was all gobbledygook to her.

She hadn't found anything that even suggested power surges could affect humans. But you couldn't expect a power company to actually admit something like that, could you?

If she hadn't fought with Luke, at least she'd have someone to share her failure with. She regretted the fight.

Or did she? He was obviously a flake. The last thing she needed was to get mixed up with a flake.

Still, she felt completely alone now. She hadn't had any more nightmare episodes, but she still felt encased in a glass shell.

When her parents asked about her day, it took all her will just to find the meaningless words to answer them.

It was a relief when her dad started talking about work. "I'll have to go back to the plant again tonight," he said to her mother, sighing as he cut up the sausage her mom cooked just for him. Apparently the power surges were growing more troublesome.

"Happens almost every night between ten and eleven," her father said, frowning. "But we can't seem to figure out what's causing them or where they're originating. Last night's surge was especially powerful. Almost blew out the transformer."

Suddenly Mandy sat up straight. Her dad's words had sparked a brain flash. A rush of shivery energy made her stomach flutter. She had an idea how to find out exactly what happened during a power surge.

She could hardly wait for the meal to be over. But once their plates were empty, her mother started talking — some amazing case at the hospital where she worked as a nurse.

"It's like a miracle," her mom said, her blue eyes alive with wonder. "This kid broke his arm two days ago and today he comes in demanding his cast off. Arrogant little jerk with one of those silly shaved heads. Starts spouting off, telling the doctors they don't know beans about medicine. Only his language was more crude, if you know what I mean."

Mandy's mom shook her head. "But .the strange part is, his arm really was healed. Completely. As if it had never been broken at all. Strangest thing I've ever seen in my life."

Mandy couldn't contain her curiosity. "What was his name, Mom?"

"Oh, honey, I don't know. He wasn't my patient originally," Mrs. Durgin said, beginning to stack dishes. "Nobody you'd know, anyway. He was one of those grungy-looking kids with all the leather."

Mandy's heart began to thud. Surely there couldn't be any connection. Could there? She pictured Quentin's hangers-on.

Was one of them wearing a cast? She hadn't noticed, but then Quentin had taken most of her attention. She suppressed a shiver at the memory.

Mandy stacked the dishwasher and then went to her dad's study. He was looking over some of the manuals that had been so meaningless to her.

"Dad," Mandy said, "there's a meteor shower tonight and I told the kids from the astronomy club that I'd ask if I could borrow your video camera to record it."

"I guess," he said, just as she had hoped. "Just don't let anyone else use it. The battery should be fully charged, but you better check it."

Elated at her success, Mandy gave her dad a kiss on the forehead. "I should be home by midnight," she said cheerfully. "Though it might run a little late."

Up in her room, she stared at the phone, biting her lip. After she'd carefully rehearsed what she was going to say, she called Luke.

He wasn't home. His machine answered. This, in a way, made things easier. "Sorry about earlier," Mandy said breezily, as if it meant nothing to her. "I've got an idea — a theory. We can test it tonight. Please call me as soon as you get in."

She put on a sweatshirt and her old running shoes, checked the camera battery, and collected the tripod. Then there was nothing to do but wait for Luke to call.

And think. An hour passed and Luke didn't call. Was he still mad?

Mandy was getting frantic. Her idea was beginning to seem more dangerous than smart. Her stomach was in knots. She couldn't go alone.

But what else could she do? Call it off? Go another night? She'd already told her father she was going and she had the video camera. She could hardly tell him the meteor shower had been postponed.

Mandy called Luke again. Maybe he hadn't checked his answering machine.

"Hi, this is Luke. I'm not home . . ."

Mandy began to put the phone down. Where could he be?

She gritted her teeth in frustration and put the receiver back to her ear just as the beep sounded.

"It's Mandy. Again. I've got a video camera to record astronomical anomalies for the astronomy club. Meet me on Old High Street — you know where — if you're still interested. The, uh, phenomenon is supposed to start at ten, so I'm leaving now. It's nine-thirty."

She hung up without saying good-bye. She was too angry. He was probably hanging out with his so-called buds while she was risking her life.

Though she probably couldn't blame Luke for not being a mind reader. Maybe she should leave a clearer message. But what if his parents heard it? Or his obnoxious brother?

Mandy went downstairs with her gear. Her father was just leaving to go to the power plant. "Do you want a ride?" he asked.

"Uh, no. Some kids are coming for me," she said. She couldn't let him drive her up there and see that no one else was around.

Mandy waited for his car to turn the corner before she headed out. As she started up the deserted street, a feeling of dread weighed her down. Would Luke understand her message? Would he come?

The night got darker when she turned onto Old High Street. The moon was obscured by clouds, and the only streetlight was on the pole where the high-tension wires crossed.

The streetlight shone brighter for an instant. As if welcoming her with its cold glow.

Mandy forced herself to keep going. The muscles across her shoulders were tight.

She kept to the side of the road where the shadows were deepest, but still she felt exposed, like eyes dogged her every step. The gravel and sand crunching under her feet sounded as loud as explosives.

As she neared the rise, the crackle of the wires buzzed along her nerves. She felt like an unseen electrical force was settling over her.

Trembling slightly, she skirted the circle of illumination from the streetlight as if the light itself might snare her.

Her breath rapid, Mandy paused, peering down the dark road in hopes of seeing Luke. But she knew by now he wasn't coming.

It was getting late. She didn't have much time. Turning her back on the road, Mandy switched on her flashlight and waded into the tall weeds, wincing as stickers caught on her jeans.

She wanted to set up well off the road, where the camera would have the widest view. If only she could shake off the sensation that someone was watching.

It was so dark she couldn't see what she was tripping over. Surely this was far enough. Mandy stopped and looked back. With sinking heart she realized she hadn't come far at all.

Mandy wasn't sure exactly where to point the camera. So she wanted to be certain the lens would take in a wide area around the high-tension wires and the spot where Luke had blacked out.

At last she found a likely location. She tramped down the weeds as best she could and set up the tripod. Her fingers fumbled attaching the camera and she nearly dropped it. She had to wait for her fingers to stop shaking so she could try again.

Finally she got the camera secured. But the ground was uneven and the tripod kept threatening to fall over.

Mandy's heart tripped faster as the seconds ticked by. She scraped and kicked at the ground in a furious effort to even it out.

The crackle and sputter of the wires plucked at her skin. Was the noise getting more intense? She kept looking around nervously, jumping at shadows.

At last the tripod seemed shakily balanced.

Mandy wished more than anything she could leave. But she didn't dare leave her dad's camera. He'd kill her if anything happened to it.

She hunkered down among the weeds, as hidden as she could get, hardly even conscious of the gnats and mosquitoes.

Suddenly an arc, like miniature lightning, bridged the wires. Mandy stared, mesmerized, too frightened to move.

The sputtering increased. It sounded like a billion angry bees popping in hot fat.

And then there was a new sound.

A rustling behind her in the woods.

The noise stopped.

Mandy strained her ears. Every nerve in her skin was tingling.

There was a snap, like a twig breaking. The crunch of footsteps on layers of dead leaves. Something — no — some*one* was coming.

Or was it her imagination? With the buzzing, sparking wires jangling her nerves, Mandy couldn't tell what she was hearing.

She felt wrung out with fright.

She didn't know what was real and what wasn't.

From the road, the wires crackled louder. Sparks rose like bright stars in the darkness.

Behind her, leaves crunched in the woods. A foot shuffled. A twig snapped.

Mandy clamped a hand to her mouth to stifle a cry.

A shower of sparks lit up the night.

Something groaned.

Mandy swung her head and saw a strange figure lurch out of the woods. No more than twenty feet away.

It was headed right for her. As the sparks faded, the night went dark again and she couldn't see anything.

Desperate to escape, Mandy tripped across the weedy ground, toward the road. Her heart pounded in her ears. Had she been spotted?

The lurching footsteps seemed to be getting closer.

The wires sparked again. In the flash of light Mandy saw a shaggy head and long arms reaching for her.

The air split with a sound like a shot.

Mandy screamed.

A huge weight slammed her into the ground.

Chapter Thirteen

Luke's eyes snapped open. It was dark. There was a dry, tickly taste in his mouth. His hand throbbed. Something was crawling over his ear. The back of his head ached.

Memory flooded back. He'd been chasing some ghostlike creature. Only it wasn't a ghost. Luke knew it wasn't anything from this Earth.

He had almost caught it. And then — nothing. Blankness. For hours.

Sitting up, he was pretty sure he hadn't been moved from the spot where he'd fallen. His leg was twisted under him and he was stiff everywhere.

He spit the leaf litter out of his mouth and felt the back of his head where it hurt. His skull felt smooth, not even a lump.

Luke hauled himself up and leaned against a tree, trying to get his bearings. There was no chance of following the creature's trail. It was too dark. Trying would only spoil what trace there might be left.

Luke was determined to come back at first light. Somehow he would track these things down.

Meantime, he had to figure out where he was.

Holding his throbbing head, Luke tried to think. He had been running deeper into the woods when he had fallen — or had been knocked out.

So, reason had it, if he just turned around and started walking, he should come to the road.

Luke took a breath. His legs felt wobbly. He placed one foot in front of the other.

As soon as he took a step he felt it again. Eyes watching him.

It was a cold, detached gaze. It reminded him of the way a scientist might study a rat in a maze. Only he was the rat and the night was the maze.

Luke felt his anger rise. He'd show them.

Somehow.

Doubt tightened his chest as Luke tensed his shoulders and started through the woods.

It wasn't long before he knew he was headed in the right direction. Even through the dense trees, he could see the sparking of the wires at the high-tension junction.

Luke's heart leaped at the sound of something in the underbrush. Was it one of them? He tried to move faster and quieter. Maybe there was still a chance he could catch one.

The wires sparked and Luke got a shadowed glimpse of the creature.

He started to run, close enough now that the noise didn't matter. Its dark outline was just ahead. Within reach.

Luke launched himself into the air in a full tackle.

Light sparked off the high-tension lines. There was a sharp crack, like a rifle report.

Then a scream.

Luke's body slammed into something soft. Warm. Human. Sleek hair filled his mouth.

"Mandy?" Luke instantly rolled away, dumbfounded.

"Luke?"

He couldn't see her face. But it was Mandy's voice. She sounded shaky but relieved.

"What are you doing here? I thought you were —" He stopped, unsure what to say. "I didn't know it was you."

"You didn't get my message?" Mandy asked, still a little breathless and confused.

"No. I —" Luke broke off. Suddenly he could see Mandy's frightened face. There was a steady glow in the air.

The air had gone still and quiet. He could no longer hear the angry sputter of the wires.

His eyes flashed to the high-tension lines. His blood froze at what he saw there.

There was a shimmering glow edging the wires. The air began to thicken. It felt charged with electricity.

"Mandy, we've got to get out of here. Now!" His voice sounded hollow. Luke grabbed her hand and they both raced for the road.

Brambles grabbed at their clothes. Rocks seemed to leap up to trip them. Mandy stumbled and Luke yanked her up, never breaking stride.

Then the air around them seemed to shift and part. Sound returned. The crackle of the wires burst loud and menacing again, as if somehow alive.

And there was a new sound. A deep hum filled the night. Luke felt the hum reach into his heart and make it vibrate. His teeth chattered uncontrollably.

An unseen charge coalesced around them like a cage. It clung like poisonous static to his clothes and slipped nooselike around his neck. The hum filled his ears and made his brain ache.

The air shimmered as the hum moved through it, homing in on them. He didn't know which way to run.

Mandy screamed. "Luke! Look!"

Mandy's terrified eyes were fixed on the sky. Luke already knew what he would see.

The stars were disappearing, winking out one by one.

Blackness spread rapidly across the sky, consuming the stars, the moon, everything in its path.

The blackness closed over them like a thick, invisible cloak. Luke tried to shout, but all he managed was a croak.

His sight narrowed as the charged darkness stole his eyes.

The edges of his vision crumpled. Mandy disappeared.

He felt his feet leave the ground.

He was suspended in nothingness. And then he was — nothing.

Chapter Fourteen

Mandy heard a groan.

The groan came again, and she realized she was the one making such an awful sound.

Awareness flooded back, slamming her like a tidal wave. Mandy sat up and looked around wildly, seeing nothing but darkness.

"Luke?" She was amazed that sound emerged. Fear had her throat in a choke hold. "Luke!"

Nothing. Then there was a furtive stirring nearby. Mandy hadn't thought she could feel more scared, but she could. Her heart was pounding its way out of her chest. She didn't dare breathe.

Something scraped at the ground and there was a grunt, like a large animal rooting around. "Luuuke!" she shrieked.

"Mandy?" Luke's frightened voice came out

of the dark, close to her. "Are you hurt? What's wrong?"

"Luke!" She felt almost giddy with relief. "I thought I was alone. I can't see anything. Do you know where we are? What happened? Do you remember?"

"I think we're in the woods," said Luke. "I feel leaves and twigs under me."

He was right. Mandy began to make out the shapes of trees. She smelled damp earth. As her fear receded, she felt stones poking her and pine needles prickling her ankles.

And she was cold. Cold to the bone.

"I can't remember a thing after — the — blackness lifted us," Luke continued in an uncertain, wavery voice. "It seems like all that was just a second ago, like nothing happened in between. Like I was switched off somehow."

Suddenly Mandy had a horrible thought. "What time is it?!" she cried. "My parents are going to kill me!"

Luke had a watch with a luminous face. When he pushed up his jacket sleeve to look, she could see where he was. The sight of him, even though he was just a black shape, calmed her further.

"It's two A.M. We lost four hours. Just like the first time."

Mandy shuddered. "I suppose it was the

power surge. It must have nearly fried our brains."

"Huh? What are you talking about?"

"It was a tremendous power surge. Obviously. I mean, you know that. You were there. It's clear the power surge put us into a fugue state," Mandy insisted. "Kind of a brain seizure. Luckily the effects seem temporary."

"Oh, right," said Luke. "And then we sleepwalked here and decided to nap on the damp ground."

"You don't have to be sarcastic," Mandy spat. "I suppose you think it was aliens," she said with sarcasm of her own.

Luke didn't respond.

"Electrical fields are known to do strange things to the human brain," she said, forcing her voice into a reasonable tone. "Our brain activity, after all, is just a series of electrical impulses. A strong surge like that can scramble those impulses, overloading the switches."

She got to her feet and briskly brushed off her jeans. "Our minds went into shock. Shut down our consciousness as a survival mechanism. We wandered mechanically until the effect wore off. Then we collapsed, probably slept for a while to regenerate energy and — here we are."

Luke was silent for a beat. "Interesting theory, Mandy, but there's a problem. I saw something very strange in the woods behind the power-line junction several hours before this happened," he said finally. "It was some kind of living thing. And it was not human."

"What was it then?" she challenged. "What did it look like? A noncarbon-based life-form, I suppose."

Luke ignored her tone. "It was shimmery. Almost invisible. As if it was at the edge of what humans can see."

Mandy was glad Luke couldn't see her eyes rolling. She tried to keep her voice even. She didn't want him to stalk off mad and leave her in the woods.

"Luke, our brains have taken severe shocks. We've both been subject to excruciating hallucinations."

Quentin's leering face flashed into her mind for a searing, horrible instant. Mandy faltered, suddenly breathless. But Luke didn't notice.

"Yeah. Well, this hallucination came after me because I found something strange," he said defiantly. "An artifact. Some clear substance I'd never seen before."

"Oh? Where is it?" asked Mandy archly, covering the shakiness of her thoughts. "Can I see it?"

She knew he'd have some excuse why she couldn't.

"The — creature — shot something at me. It destroyed the thing I found. Reduced it to powder. Which I can show you once we get out of here. Plus, I've got a nasty blister on my hand where the beam hit me."

"I see. A blister."

Luke went on. "I chased it. Almost caught it, too. They don't move through Earth's atmosphere very well. I think our air tires them. Or maybe it's the gravity."

"But you didn't catch it, did you?"

"No. There must have been another one out there waiting. It shot me from behind, I think. Some kind of stun gun. I was out for hours. When I came out of the woods and found you, I had just woken up."

"Luke, listen to yourself," Mandy pleaded. Her patience was disappearing fast. "Do you know how crazy this sounds?"

Luke sighed. "Yeah. But I know what I saw. It wasn't a hallucination."

"Look, in a way, I sympathize," Mandy said. "Given the trillions of stars and the likelihood of billions of solar systems, chances are good for the existence of life elsewhere in the universe, and it seems possible that some of that life could be intelligent."

"Well, well," Luke said. "A major concession."

"Not exactly," Mandy corrected. "Any possible civilizations are so many light-years distant that it's unlikely anyone in Earth's lifetime will ever meet them, much less in our *own* lifetime. The government has been searching for alien life for years and never found one scrap of evidence. And now you think they've decided to plunk down in Greenfield and come after us? Our chances of winning the lottery are more likely than that."

Luke was silent for a moment. But Mandy knew she hadn't convinced him.

"What were you doing out there anyway, Mandy? Why were you hanging around the power lines at ten o'clock at night?"

"Trying to record objective evidence," she told him. "I borrowed my dad's video camera and set it up to tape what happened during a power surge."

"Really," Luke responded thoughtfully. He was quiet for a moment. "Hey, we'd better start for home," he said suddenly. "Any idea which way to go?"

Mandy looked at the sky, glad to change the subject. "There's the moon. It's setting in the southwest, so that way must be east. The road should be east."

Without a flashlight, the going was slow. The undergrowth was a tangle of bushes, many with thorns. The dark was so complete they kept walking into low branches and tripping over rocks and roots.

Conversation was limited to grunts and curses and an occasional "Ouch, that must have hurt" and "Are you okay?"

But eventually they came out behind the power plant, scratched and exhausted. The plant was ringed with lights.

Luke's hair was full of bits of leaves and pine needles, and there was a dirty scratch over one eye.

"If I look half as bad as you," Mandy said, "I'm going to be in even bigger trouble than I already thought."

"You'll need to clean up a little," Luke agreed.

Suddenly it began to drizzle. "Oh, no!" Mandy cried. "My father's camera. We'd better hurry."

"Right," said Luke. He sounded eager. "I'll be curious to see what's on it."

Mandy was cold and exhausted and achy. The thought of going back to the power-line junction filled her with dread. But Luke set off briskly. Mandy had trouble keeping up with him.

It was past three when the tall metal poles with their sputtering wires and the single streetlight came into view.

Without needing to speak, they both stopped. Mandy's feet felt rooted to the pavement.

"I don't know," she said. "Maybe we should come back in daylight. I can think of something to tell my father."

"No way," Luke insisted. "I can imagine how my dad would react. I can do this in a second. You stay here, I'll be right back."

Mandy was tempted. But she couldn't let Luke do it alone. "I'm with you. But let's do it quickly."

She gripped his hand and they dashed together into the weeds.

"There's the camera," Mandy said with relief. "It's still recording."

Luke snatched it up, tripod and all. He got the tripod folded together without detaching the camera.

Once they were back on the road, Luke seemed to forget everything but the video camera.

He stopped right under the buzzing menace of the power lines. He unhitched the camera, handing Mandy the tripod.

"This has a playback feature, doesn't it?" he asked eagerly, rewinding the tape and hitting a button.

"Luke," Mandy said pointedly, "I'd like to get a little farther from those wires."

He looked at her, surprised. "They're done with us for tonight," he said.

"They?" Mandy felt a dose of irritation mix in with her nervousness.

"Uh, the power surge, I mean," Luke told her. "It's over."

"Still, I prefer not to take any more chances," Mandy said, tugging his arm and urging him along.

But as soon as they turned off Old High Street, Luke insisted on stopping. They huddled close, looking into the small viewing screen as the tape flickered into life.

The first image wobbled, Mandy's arm appearing as a dark shadow as she bent to level the tripod. Then came the streaks of light from the sparking power lines.

"Oh!" Mandy couldn't believe what she was seeing.

The darkness gathered over the sparking, sputtering power lines. They watched in horrified fascination as it seemed to grow, sucking power from the lines.

The dark blot began to move toward the camera, devouring everything in its path. Even on tape, the inky blackness seemed like a living presence. The leaves on the trees trembled and went still.

Mandy gripped Luke's arm as the hum reverberated in her brain once again, tuning to the beat of her heart. And then, just as she was about to snap the camera off in panic, two figures ran into the picture.

It was them! Luke and Mandy. Legs pumping without getting anywhere. Their mouths open in soundless terror. And suddenly they both stopped in midstride.

Mandy thought she could see the life drain out of her own eyes.

The darkness swirled over them and slowly descended, enveloping them.

Their bodies went limp but didn't fall.

And then they began to rise.

Mandy watched in disbelief as she and Luke rose straight into the air.

No mistake — the illumination from the sparking power lines was perfect, the focus clear.

The tape showed them rising right out of the picture, into the sky.

Chapter Fifteen

Luke gaped in horrified awe as the night settled back to normal on the tape.

Minus two unconscious people.

The wires stopped their crazy sputtering. The light changed.

"The moon's back," Luke whispered.

"What?" Mandy asked. Her voice was dazed and small.

Luke gestured at the running tape. "The light. You can see moonlight again."

Mandy made a choking noise. Luke could imagine how hard this was for her. Worse even than for him. No way you could put this particular phenomenon down to a "power surge."

"We'll show it to my dad," Mandy said, stabbing the button that stopped the tape. "There's got to be some explanation. Come on."

Luke felt a little weird about going home with Mandy at three in the morning. But he definitely wanted to hear her father's explanation.

Mandy's front door flew open before she had a chance to turn the knob. "Where have you been?" demanded her father, looming over them both.

Mandy's mother appeared beside him. The anger in her face changed when she caught sight of her disheveled and dirt-streaked daughter.

"What happened to you? Are you all right?" Her eyes turned accusingly to Luke. "Who *is* this?"

"I'm Luke Ingram, Mrs. Durgin," he said, stepping forward — though every muscle in his body yearned for flight. "We've had a terrible experience, but this tape will explain everything." He gestured at the tape in Mandy's hand.

"Tape!?" Mr. Durgin's face turned incredulous. "Do you know what time it is? Mandy, your mother's been frantic. I want an explanation!"

"Were you in an accident?" Mrs. Durgin asked, pulling Mandy inside and examining her face.

Luke, forgotten for the moment, stepped into the house. He wished he could sink beneath the floorboards. But as soon as they saw the videotape, this torture would be over.

Then they would realize that something horribly strange was happening in their town.

Ignoring her parents' questions, Mandy ran down the hall to the TV room.

Her outraged mom and dad had no choice but to follow. Luke stood in the doorway while Mandy pushed in the tape and turned the VCR on.

She stepped back with a flourish, looking at her parents' faces rather than at the screen. But her parents' expressions didn't change.

Luke watched the screen in confusion. All the hope and energy drained out of him.

"Mandy. Look," he said softly.

She turned to the screen and saw what he saw.

Nothing. Static. Gray mist.

"It's got to be here!" Mandy cried. She pressed the button for fast forward.

More static.

She jammed the button again. Nothing.

The proof had disappeared.

Chapter Sixteen

Getting out of Mandy's house had been a nightmare. Her parents' furious disbelief, his tongue-tied shock, Mandy's frantic attempts to explain the unexplainable — it was all a mess.

And he still had to run the gauntlet of his own parents. Luke stopped in front of his house and sighed. It looked like every light was blazing.

That image of him and Mandy rising into the air kept taking hold of his mind. It was hard to think of anything else.

But he made a supreme effort as he opened the front door. Luke winced at the sight of his parents' faces, strained with worry.

"Where have you been?" his father demanded.

"Have you seen Jeff?" his mother asked.

Lucky for him, Jeff was still out. So his own

explanation of falling asleep while watching a meteor shower went over surprisingly well. In minutes he was in his room.

He knew he'd never sleep, but he got ready for bed and lay down. His brain was whirling with images that flitted just out of reach. No matter how he strained he couldn't get them to come clear.

A strange lethargy took hold of him. His body began to feel heavy. He was sinking deep into the mattress. His arms and legs seemed detached from him, like chunks of thick wood rather than flesh.

The weight was pulling him down, down into sleep.

And then suddenly he was yanked into consciousness. Every cell in his body was shrieking with alarm.

The room was dark. His mouth was dry and his body felt clammy like he'd been sleeping too deeply for too long.

But now something had awakened him. His heart pounded.

There was menace in the room. A presence, just beyond sight. A sense of evil so palpable, Luke felt it saturate the air and seep through his pores, poisoning him.

He began to shiver as the horror of it settled in his chest like a black spill. It spread quickly, smothering his lungs, stopping his heart.

Luke lay helpless. His breath wheezed painfully. His heart struggled like a trapped bird.

"What?" he managed to choke out. "What do you want?"

The air around him shifted. Luke could almost see it. He felt a weight on his rib cage. A face appeared, hanging in the air above him.

"I thought you'd never ask," it said.

An evil more depraved than Luke had ever believed in shone from this face. It was at once soulless and supremely confident.

"I've become rather handsome, wouldn't you agree?" asked Quentin, grinning as his body materialized, seated cross-legged on Luke's chest.

Quentin's skin was pale but perfectly smooth. His brown hair was now lustrous and thick, with a slight wave. His teeth were white and straight. He had a beautiful smile.

Luke thought he had never seen anything more terrifying.

Quentin rose. He went to sit at Luke's desk chair across the room. Although Luke felt the weight lift, his chest seemed permanently compressed.

Luke stared. His senses were finely honed by fear. He could see starlight glint in Quentin's still, colorless eyes. He could smell evil as cloying as heavy perfume. As undeniable as death.

Luke could hear the healthy pump of Quentin's heart from across the room.

And Luke could feel the greedy tug of Quentin's life force as it sucked the vitality from his own.

Quentin noted Luke's abject horror with satisfaction. "All this," he said, indicating his new look, "doesn't come cheap." He chuckled softly. "For you anyway.

"But that's not really why I'm here," Quentin continued. "There's something I want you to see." His eyes gleamed with anticipation. "No particular reason to show you this, really. Just for pleasure."

He raised finely arched eyebrows at Luke's motionless form. "But then that's really what life is all about, isn't it, Luke boy? The pursuit of pleasure. Some people limit their pleasures to power, wealth, sex. Others, like myself, are more imaginative. Watch."

As Quentin spoke, Luke was slammed against the headboard of his bed. He felt as if a glowing ball of pure energy had hurtled across his room and embedded itself full force in his stomach.

The breath was knocked from his body. He groaned, involuntarily shutting his eyes. Immediately he was overcome by a powerful dizziness.

His eyes snapped open, too late. His familiar room had vanished.

Luke was no longer in his bed. He was looking down at his own lifeless body. It was strapped to a gurney. Other than a fretful helpless dread, the body aroused little interest in him.

Something else demanded his attention. What it was he didn't yet know.

Luke couldn't really see where he was. His vision was limited. The edges softened to a blurred mist. Beyond the mist was some sort of activity. Others were there, occupied with something.

Anxiety rose in him like a tide. He needed to know what they were doing. Who *they* were.

His eyes pried at the fog, straining to penetrate it. Suddenly the mist swirled, dissolved, and re-formed.

Luke's field of vision had abruptly changed. He was looking down on a strange scene. Humanoids, strangely familiar, were bending over something. Their bodies obscured its identity.

The white figures wore clinging silvery garments that shimmered as they moved. They were oddly sexless, like dolls, with hairless heads. He couldn't see their faces, but they seemed very intent on something.

Frustrated, Luke tried to move his head or whatever it was that contained his eyes, but this was impossible. It seemed he was being permitted only to see the backs of their heads.

Then one of them turned. Recognition hit Luke with full force. He saw the bulging forehead, the multifaceted housefly eyes, the puttylike nose.

These were the creatures from his neardrowning vision in the quarry pool.

His mind reeled. What was happening to him? Was any of this real?

The group shifted. Suddenly he could see the object of their intense attention.

Mandy.

She lay motionless on the gurney, clothed only in a long T-shirt that reached to midthigh. Wires sprouted from her head. Only her eyes moved, darting from side to side, twitching in panic.

Piercingly blue, Mandy's eyes were the sole points of color visible. They were a startling brilliance in the weirdly colorless scene of silver and white.

Luke knew she couldn't see him. He tried to call her name but found he couldn't make a sound.

Several of the creatures held long, silver instruments. Like the one Quentin had been toying with at the quarry park, with a slender handle ending in a polished ten-inch needle point.

Luke's helplessness infuriated him. He wanted to scream, to lash out in all directions with his fists. But all he could do was watch.

There was another stir among the creatures. They moved to make room for a newcomer. Luke tried to follow the direction of their gaze but could not.

And then Quentin stepped into his line of vision.

The new movie-star-handsome version of Quentin stepped up to the side of the gurney. Pressing himself against it, Quentin leaned over Mandy.

Her eyes widened in a vast blue sea of terror and revulsion. Her chest began to rise and fall rapidly.

Even in his disembodied state, Luke could feel the waves of joyful evil emanating from Quentin. Luke knew with absolute certainty that this was the part Quentin wanted him to see.

Quentin licked his forefinger with an impossibly long tongue. He reached out and touched Mandy's toe, then trailed his finger along her foot, tracing further to the outline of her calf. He lifted the hem of her T-shirt.

Hot and cold waves broke over Luke. He felt he was drowning in an ocean of pain.

A harsh whispery sound rose from the humanoids. One of them raised a supple, boneless-looking arm. He seemed to be gesturing to Quentin to stop.

But the motion was hesitant. As if the creature was reluctant to offend someone dangerous.

Quentin shrugged. Letting Mandy's T-shirt fall back into place, he withdrew his hand.

Splaying out his hand, Quentin licked his fingers one by one, staring into Mandy's face as he did.

Then Quentin turned to one of the humanoids. He took the silver wand from its hands.

Carefully he poised the sharp point of the instrument over the swell of Mandy's chest. He spoke. The words were perfectly audible to Luke.

"Remember Mandy," he said. "If I can't have you . . ." Quentin paused. He grinned and touched the tip of his horrible tongue to his nose. "If I can't have you, nobody can."

In a flash, Quentin plunged the long silvery needle deep into Mandy's chest, piercing her heart.

Luke howled.

Darkness rushed in and swallowed him whole.

Chapter Seventeen

The scream hurt her ears. The piercing noise ripped through her head from one side to the other.

Mandy needed to make it stop. She twisted, trying to find its source in the dense fog that shrouded her. Was it a child? An animal?

The awful noise came again and Mandy's hand flailed out, knocking against her bedside table. She came fully awake. Her phone was ringing.

She grabbed it up. Her heart was pounding. "Hello?"

"Mandy? Is that you?"

"Luke?" Mandy frowned. She could see cool bluish light through her window. Absently she rubbed her chest. It ached. "Of course it's me. Who else? This is my number, isn't it?"

She felt disoriented. Her body was bathed in

sweat, as if she'd just run a race. Her eyes felt gritty.

She heard a sharp exhale of relief through the phone. "Mandy, are you all right?"

"All right?" Mandy squinted at her alarm clock. "It's six o'clock in the morning. I've only had two hours sleep." Actually she felt like she hadn't had any. "Of course I'm not all right."

"Thank God. I mean, I'm sorry I woke you. It must have been a dream." Luke's voice was shaky. "A horrible dream. I'll talk to you later."

An image flitted through Mandy's mind. It was gone before she could catch it, but it left her shuddering with revulsion. She clutched the phone. Suddenly she couldn't bear to be left alone. "Luke, wait."

"Yes? I'm still here."

Mandy's jaw locked. Icy sweat trickled down her spine. "What dream?" she wanted to ask. But her lips wouldn't work.

"Mandy?" There was a sharp note of worry in Luke's voice.

Mandy forced her jaw apart. But suddenly she didn't want to know anything about his dream. "Luke, you know that UFO meeting, the notice we saw in the cafe?"

"Sure." His voice was guarded.

Mandy realized he had intended to go without telling her. "I'd like to go."

"But I thought —"

"No, I don't think we were abducted by aliens," Mandy said quickly, "but I think some people might show up who have had experiences similar to ours. If there's a group of us, maybe we could go to the power-plant people."

"Okay." Luke's tone was carefully neutral.

It needled Mandy. "Come on, Luke. You don't really think we were lifted into the sky. You can't. There was nothing on that tape. We must have hallucinated the whole thing."

"It's okay, Mandy," said Luke. "I think it's a good idea to go to that meeting."

But Mandy felt a need to convince him. "We obviously had a joint hallucination caused by our brains' inability to deal with the sensory overload caused by the electrical surge," she said.

"A levitation hallucination," commented Luke drily.

Mandy thought of what had happened when her phone had rung. It was a perfect example.

"It happens all the time in dreams and we think nothing of it. Like when your alarm clock goes off and you don't want to get up. So your dream turns it into something else. Fantastic things sometimes."

"Sure," said Luke. "The only difference is we were awake. And we both had exactly the same hallucination. Excuse me, *dream.*"

"Either that or we were abducted by aliens from outer space," Mandy snapped sarcastically.

"There's one thing I don't get," Luke said.

"Only one thing?"

Luke ignored her attitude. "If you're certain this has to do with the power plant and the power surges, why didn't you ask your dad about it? Why didn't you tell him the truth last night?"

Mandy winced. It had been difficult, scrambling for a story to satisfy her parents.

"I was trying to calm them," she said archly. "Telling them we blanked out for several hours and then saw ourselves levitating into the sky on a blank tape didn't seem like a good idea at four o'clock in the morning."

Instead she had spun out a tale about strange lights that had so intrigued them they lost track of time.

In the end, since Luke and Mandy were obviously sober and unhurt, her parents had grudgingly accepted it. They even commiserated with Mandy over her incompetence with the video camera.

"Go back to sleep," Luke said now. "I'll come by for you this afternoon, three o'clock."

But Mandy was not used to sleeping in the daytime. She kept waking up, clammy with sweat, her heart thumping erratically. Each time, she felt hollowed out by some nameless dread.

The disturbing dreams fled with consciousness. But she could feel them lurking at the edges of her mind, waiting for sleep to drag her under again.

She tried to get up. But again and again, exhaustion overwhelmed her before she could summon the strength.

Finally one of the dreams propelled her upright. She sat, gasping and shaking with fear. She couldn't remember a thing. Somehow that made the fear worse.

She threw her feet over the side of the bed. When the trembling had subsided enough to let her stand, she grabbed her robe and headed for the shower.

Mandy stood under the water for a long time, letting it beat over her. But long after the traces of sweat were washed away, she still felt dirty.

The water had begun to lose its heat when she felt something on the back of her neck. It slithered across the top of her spine like a worm. At first she thought it was nothing, just the sudden cooling of the water.

Then it seemed to burrow under her skin. There wasn't pain exactly. Slick and slimy, it wriggled between the cells of her skin.

Mandy screamed and slapped at herself. But

she couldn't reach it. She felt the thing dive more vigorously into her flesh. Like it was seeking a way into her bloodstream. Once there, it would multiply, feeding on her blood.

Driven by panic, Mandy scratched and tore at the back of her neck.

Then nothing. The itchy, burrowing, slithering feeling was gone.

Mandy grabbed the back of her neck with both hands. The skin felt smooth. She pressed her fingers along the area over and around her spine but felt no bumps or yielding, snakelike ribbons.

She shuddered so hard that drops of water went flying from her body. There was no way she could have imagined such a thing.

Then a horrible thought occurred to her. Mandy scrambled out of the tub, almost slipping as she lunged to the mirror. Grabbing a towel, she cleared away the condensation. But by the time she positioned her hand mirror to see the back of her neck, both mirrors had fogged again.

Pulling on her thick terry robe, Mandy stumbled to her bedroom. She positioned herself in front of the full-length mirror and held up the hand mirror. There were red welts on the back of her neck! She stared in horror.

Mandy dashed back to the bathroom. She ejected the razor from her shaver. Hand trembling, she pulled her hair aside and held the twin-blade cartridge over her spine, ready to cut the thing out of her. But the mirror was still too blurry.

Back in her bedroom, Mandy finally came to her senses.

The red welts looked like scratch marks where she had dug at herself with her nails. There weren't any holes or tiny puncture marks that she could see. There was no sign that anything had ever been on her neck.

And if there had been a parasite it was long gone. It would be swimming merrily in her bloodstream. By now it might have released a hundred young maggots, swarming to every tiny vein and capillary in her body.

Her head swung to the clock. Two-thirty. Luke would be here in half an hour. She couldn't wait that long. Mandy snatched up the phone. If she got his answering machine, she'd scream.

But Luke answered.

"Luke, come over right now," she said and hung up. Then she sat on the side of the bed, hugging her knees and rocking.

By the time Luke came, Mandy was dressed and sitting outside, waiting on her front steps. He was slightly out of breath from having run all the way.

Mandy rose. "Take a look at the back of my

neck," she demanded before he could ask any questions. She lifted her hair and bent her head. "What do you see?"

Luke lifted a few strands she had missed. The brush of his fingers on her neck sent a sensation down her spine. The sheer normalcy of the feeling had a calming effect.

Suddenly the whole worm thing seemed so nuts she wanted to giggle.

"I don't see a thing," said Luke, mystified. "It looks a little red maybe, like you scratched it."

Mandy handed him the magnifying glass she had brought down. It might seem crazy now, but just a few minutes ago it had seemed essential. So what was the harm? "Take a close look with this."

"What am I looking for?"

"Just look."

Luke took the magnifying glass. He was silent while he examined her neck carefully.

"Everything looks fine, Mandy," he said finally. "Although maybe you scratched it too hard. The skin seems a bit raw. But not broken. What's going on?"

She sighed deeply. Sinking back down on the steps, she pulled Luke beside her. "You're not going to believe this," she said.

But of course he did. When she finished, Luke took up the magnifying glass again. This time he gently pulled aside her hair himself.

Mandy closed her eyes and gave herself up to the warm, stirring feelings his touch roused. It seemed so long since she had felt anything pleasant.

"No puncture marks, not even tiny ones," Luke concluded, returning her magnifying glass.

"Of course not," Mandy said lazily, letting her arm brush his. A tiny current seemed to jump between them. "More electrical misfirings. It was probably worse since I had just woken up. I've heard patients who have electroshock therapy sometimes feel things crawling under their skin for months, even years after."

"Great," said Luke, getting to his feet. "It's nice to know what we have to look forward to. Come on, it's past three."

The UFO meeting was taking place in a dilapidated old convenience store that had been closed and boarded up for years. It was located on Old High Street and squatted under the high-tension power lines like a beaten dog.

The buzz of the wires set them both on edge. Mandy hesitated, unwilling to pass.

Luke took her hand. He seemed hesitant, but as soon as she squeezed back, his fingers laced comfortingly with hers. It didn't make her feel less afraid, but she pretended it did.

They edged past the junction quickly.

Strangely, Mandy's nervousness did not pass as they started down the far side of the rise toward the old store. It only increased as they got closer. Her pulse began to rise.

"Oh, no," Luke muttered disgustedly, "Jeff and his scummy friends are here."

Mandy struggled to rise out of the anxious funk that was engulfing her. She saw a milling crowd of sinister-looking skinheads hanging out in a corner of the packed-dirt parking lot. "Jeff is the one with the scary lightning tattoo?"

"My parents totally freaked when they saw that," Luke said, shaking his head. "But Jeff is out of control. He absolutely refused to say where he got it. It's kind of weird how they have no control over him. He just doesn't care."

The skinheads turned to watch them as they reached the parking lot. None of them smiled. They emanated menace.

Despite the brilliance of the sunshine, Mandy shivered. Suddenly a cold wind rushed into her. It settled inside her bones. She clutched Luke's hand like a lifeline.

All at once, the group of skinheads parted in two. Instantly Mandy recognized the source of the strange cold. Quentin was sitting on the hood of a silvery sports car.

His body had changed. He was different. His skin glowed with health. His hair sparkled in the sun. His body was supple and muscular. His smile riveted her. He was beautiful, in a terrifying way. He grinned, holding her gaze as he stroked the arm of a skinhead girl standing beside him.

The girl's bald skull was nicely shaped, but her face was sullen. She wore heavy black eye makeup and black lipstick. Her mouth looked like a wound in her pale face. LOVE was crudely tattooed on her hand.

Mandy shuddered violently.

Quentin's grin vanished. He fixed his marvelous, soulless eyes on her hand, clasped to Luke's.

Suddenly, Mandy's hand burned as if it had been plunged into dry ice. Her finger bones felt so brittle she thought they might crumble to dust. Her hand was ripped from Luke's grasp. Her fingers flamed.

Quentin raised his eyes to hers. "Remember this, Mandy?" His tongue slipped from between his lips. It slithered toward her, an impossible length.

Mandy felt an icy prickle on the back of her neck. There was a sharp piercing pain, then a cold, hurried, slippery sensation under her skin.

She shrieked wildly and clawed the back of her neck.

Quentin's laughter rang out, and the wormy

feeling left her. Mandy gasped, reduced to a shivery shell.

"Such a fine time we're having together, Mandy girl," Quentin said. "I don't know when I've had so much fun. But there's other tricks this tongue can perform. Would you like to see?"

Mandy's heart clattered against her ribs like a small, crazed beast.

Quentin strolled closer, taking his time. His eyes roved over her body.

Mandy felt spiders, dozens of them, running up her legs.

Before she could react, Quentin's tongue lashed out, purple and obscene. She jerked away, but it flashed past her ear and slashed to her left. Toward Luke.

There was a quiet snick sound, like a sharp knife through cold butter.

Luke's head tipped forward. In apparent slow motion it fell from his shoulders. There was no blood. Not immediately.

Luke's head bounced on the hard-packed earth. It rolled. Bits of dirt stuck to the truncated neck.

The head rolled up against Mandy's sandal.

She felt Luke's crisp, curly hair against her toes.

His face stared up at her.

Luke's sightless eyes were dumbfounded.

Chapter Eighteen

Mandy let out a low moan. Her eyes rolled back in her head.

Quentin and his whole creepy entourage were laughing. Unconscious, Mandy began to crumple to the ground.

Luke caught her just before she hit.

His neck hurt. He felt like he'd missed something important. Another one of those weird blackouts. Luckily this one seemed to have lasted only a moment.

Maybe no one had noticed.

"Better get her inside."

Luke jumped. He hadn't noticed how close Quentin was standing. Had he done something to Mandy?

"Might be sunstroke," Quentin whispered. There was an odd glint in his eye.

But Luke was too concerned about Mandy to wonder what it was.

"Tongue-stroke," Jeff chimed in as if he was making the wittiest remark in the world.

Luke hefted Mandy, lifting her in his arms like a child. He staggered a little, then found his rhythm and started for the building.

Halfway there, Mandy stirred. Luke's spirits rose. "Mandy?" he asked hopefully. "Can you hear me?"

Her eyes flew open. The blue jumped out at him. She looked startled, even shocked.

Luke realized how strange this must seem to her, finding herself in his arms. He started to put her down, planning to apologize and explain what had happened.

But Mandy abruptly threw her arms around his neck. She buried her head on his shoulder and began to sob.

Astonished, Luke hurried toward the building. He had to get her out of the sun.

Behind him there was an angry hiss. Mandy stiffened in his arms at the sound.

Luke looked back. Quentin was eyeing him with pure hatred. His bright, even teeth were bared in a snarl. If looks were lasers, Luke would be dead.

Mandy squirmed out of Luke's arms. She faced Quentin.

"What do you want?" she demanded, hands on hips, her jaw jutting angrily. Her knees were visibly shaking.

"Among other things "— Quentin blew her a kiss — "I want you."

Mandy's face twisted with disgust and loathing. "But *I* don't want *you*."

"It wouldn't be nearly as much fun if you did," Quentin replied, his lip curling in a sneer.

Luke felt like he should do something.

The gang of skinheads had fanned out behind Quentin, watching him eagerly. They, too, wanted him to do something. Even Jeff. Especially Jeff?

Luke's younger brother licked his lips with excitement as he waited for Luke to move.

Mandy grabbed his arm. "Let's go in, Luke," she said.

Behind them, the 'heads yelled and jeered. They moved in closer, pressing with silent menace.

Luke began to wonder if the building was a trap. He tucked Mandy's arm closer against his side. Should they run for it? But a check from side to side told him it was already too late.

The skinheads flanked them on both sides. There was nothing to do but go inside. At least inside they wouldn't be trapped alone with the gang. Other people had been going in. Normal people.

Mandy hurried up the steps, pulling Luke along. Once inside, Luke was surprised to see how many people had showed up. Chairs had been set up in rows to face what had been the front counter. More than half the seats were taken.

It was an odd collection of people. There were ordinary Greenfield citizens, curious probably. Most of them sat together in a clump, as if to protect themselves from the others.

These other people were obviously not from Greenfield. Many looked disturbed, even crazy. Some passed out handwritten pamphlets detailing their experiences. Some spoke loudly to invisible aliens.

A few even wore their version of alien dress, like they thought this was a Star Trek convention or something.

Luke's eye was drawn to an elegant woman who stood alone against a side wall, observing the room with detached amusement.

She had shiny coal-black hair and wore bright red lipstick. She wore jeans that fit like gloves and boots with high heels. And she was chomping hungrily on a Mars bar.

Luke and Mandy slipped into seats on the aisle.

There was a commotion behind them as the skinheads clattered in. Heavy boots scraped and stomped on the old wooden floor. Chairs were shoved around.

The atmosphere suddenly became a lot more tense. People looked back over their shoulders nervously.

"What are you looking at, you old fart?" The skinhead's challenge cut through the remaining murmurs of idle chatter.

Quentin stopped beside a beefy man at least twice his size. Two skinheads in black T-shirts and torn black jeans flanked Quentin on either side. He smiled wolfishly.

"Excuse me, is that seat taken?" Quentin asked, pointing to the chair the man was sitting in.

The big man, obviously not used to being intimidated, started to bristle. The four goons behind Quentin took a half step forward, almost on tiptoe with anticipation. The man shook his head, got up, and took a different seat.

As the skinheads moved into the last rows with maximum noise, Luke felt himself start a slow burn. He'd like to get one of those creeps alone. They wouldn't be quite so brave and sneering without their gang to back them up.

At the same time he was aware of a flutter of fear in his gut. Besides taking over the last rows, the skinheads had bottled up the exit.

Luke could feel the attention of the room riveted on the rear, even though everyone sat rigidly face forward. They all knew they couldn't leave.

"Well, if we're all settled, let's get started." Luke hadn't noticed the gray-ponytailed man position himself behind the store's front counter. He was an aging hippie-type, wearing wire-rim glasses, a T-shirt, baggy jeans, and beat-up sandals.

The man smiled nervously, his eyes flicking toward the rear. "I'm Alan Smith, head of Alien Watch," he said. "Alien Watch has come to your community because we have reason to believe you have visitors from beyond our solar system."

Suddenly all the skinheads began drumming the floor with their heavy boots. The noise was deafening. The old building shook. Luke felt his stomach knot while anger pumped through his veins.

Suddenly he was on his feet. "Stop it!" he yelled. "Stop it! Let him talk!"

The noise grew louder, a riot of stamping — directed at him now. Dozens of blazing eyes met Luke's. He had just given them all the excuse they needed to tear him apart.

Luke felt as if his stomach had dropped abruptly out of his body. He had played right into their hands.

But his heart was still pounding with fury. Someone had to stand up to these creeps.

A couple of the gang picked up the folding chairs in front of them and began to bang them on the floor, too, grinning with mindless glee. The noise grew so loud it sounded like a fleet of jets revving up for takeoff in the tiny building.

People covered their ears with their hands. Luke could no longer hear his own thoughts.

And then Quentin raised his hand. Instantly, the noise stopped. Quiet was restored.

The gang's attention was still fixed on Luke. Several of the boys actually seemed to be panting with anticipation, their fists clenching spasmodically.

"Luke, Luke, Luke." Quentin shook his head sadly. "As brave as he is dumb. Or as dumb as he is brave. What did you think they were going to do? Go all trembly and put their fingers over their lips?"

Luke felt a stab of white-hot anger go through him. He actually hated Quentin, he realized. Helplessly.

Quentin sighed. "And now I suppose I'll have to let them have you."

One of the gang started half out of his chair, a growl sounding deep in his chest. There was a tattoo on his forehead. It was simple, homemade-looking: HATE.

Luke became aware that everyone in the audience was looking at him sympathetically. But no one would come to his aid.

Someone probably had a cell phone, Luke hoped. Maybe the police would arrive in time.

Quentin wiggled a finger. The skinhead stayed where he was, poised for attack.

"Or," Quentin said, "there is one other solution. Right, boys?" There was a beat of silence. "RIGHT, boys?"

The skinheads murmured sullen agreement.

"Mandy," Quentin said.

"No." Luke went rigid. He cursed himself. If he hadn't been such an idiot —

"If she wants to keep you out of the loving clutches of my hair-challenged friends here —"

"No," said Luke. "Leave Mandy out of it."

Mandy stood up. She shot Luke a furious look. "I'm right here. And I will do whatever I want. You're not going to wrangle over me like two dogs over a bone." She faced Quentin. "What do you want? Spit it out."

"I want you to come sit next to me." Quentin spread his hands innocently. "That's all. Just for the duration of this interesting meeting. After that, you do what you want, with whoever you want."

"You bet I will," Mandy growled.

The skinhead with the HATE tattoo slumped heavily back in his chair, disappointed.

Mandy started to sidle out past Luke. But he couldn't let her go.

He had seen the triumphant light in Quentin's eyes when Mandy agreed.

He was planning something.

If Mandy left him now, she wouldn't be back. Luke knew it.

Looking into her eyes, as thrilling and hard as sapphires, Luke also knew he could not stop her.

WOODLAWN MIDDLE SCHOOL
6362 RFD Gilmer RD.
Long Grove, IL 60047
(847) 540-0013

Chapter Nineteen

Mandy shoved past Luke. She was furious.

Furious at Luke for blowing up and directing Quentin's attention to them again. Furious at everybody else for not doing anything. Furious most of all at Quentin and the skinheads for making normal people feel so helpless.

She was bitterly afraid. For herself, but mostly for Luke.

She walked the few steps down to Quentin's row. "Move over," she snapped. "I'm sitting on the aisle."

Quentin threw up his hands in mock supplication and slid over. His eyes traveled over her body. Mandy shuddered with revulsion and pressed her knees tightly together as she sat.

Quentin leaned close. "I love how you look in shorts," he whispered. "They leave so little to the imagination."

His breath was both hot and cold against

Mandy's ear. She tasted bile in the back of her throat. Goose bumps rose up on her bare legs.

"I don't see why one young lady should have you all to herself." The low, throaty voice came from a woman Mandy had noticed earlier, lounging against the wall.

Now, she pushed herself off the wall and sauntered toward them. She was striking-looking with her jet black hair and full, perfect lips. She didn't look much older than Mandy. But still a world apart.

The woman edged gracefully into the row and eased into the seat on Quentin's other side. "I'll just sit right here," she said in a voice like velvet.

Quentin was clearly displeased, but he didn't protest. Mandy's goose bumps subsided. Her stomach settled back into place.

"Please go on, Mr. Smith," the woman said, raising her voice only slightly. "I know we're all eager to hear your presentation. And I don't believe you'll be disturbed again."

Her voice was smooth, with a hint of threat. "Will he?" she asked, inclining her head toward Quentin.

"No," Quentin answered sourly. "No more disturbances."

Mandy heard shifting in the rows behind her, but no one said a word.

She looked up at Mr. Smith. He licked his lips

nervously and fiddled with his ponytail. "Ah, yes, as I was saying. Our group, Alien Watch, has detected activity in your area."

His eyes darted to the back of the room. Mandy braced herself for more stamping, but nothing happened. Mr. Smith cleared his throat.

"Indications include unexplained power surges, strange lights in the sky, and odd bursts of radioactivity. These things are measurable."

With an attentive audience, Smith gained confidence. He pulled an easel forward. "As you can see from my maps, you are not alone. Alien activity has also been detected here, here, and here," he said, using a pointer to indicate various places around the country.

He moved to another easel and began tapping blurry smears of light, claiming these were alien spaceships. As he grew more excited, spittle flew from his mouth.

Mandy felt disgusted and embarrassed for him. This was how rumors got started. Why was it people would rather believe the most fantastic absurdities than the logic of hard science?

"It's also likely there have been abductions." Smith looked hard at the audience, caught up now in his passion. "Some of you have probably been abducted," he continued, the words tumbling out. "You may not know you've been abducted. You may know only that your sleep is disturbed, your dreams strange and frightening. Others among you will be aware of missing time, or episodes of what you may pass off as sleepwalking. If you believe you've been abducted, come forward. Earth herself may depend on you."

Mentally, Mandy groaned. Luke, who had been twisting around every second to look at her, was now facing straight forward. Riveted.

A woman rose. She wore an elaborate arrangement of scarves around her head. "The aliens pulled out all my hair, strand by strand," she said breathlessly. She described an immense spaceship and two-headed aliens who were cloning humans from her hair.

A wild-eyed man jumped up and told how aliens had taken over his mind and let him eat nothing but Jell-O for one month, then nothing but spinach for another.

Several more people told stories of being abducted. The tales depressed Mandy. To stop them, she found herself standing up. Behind her, chairs creaked ominously. Several pairs of boots hit the floor. She saw Quentin's hand come up and the activity stopped. There was silence all around her. Luke was looking at her curiously.

"I have a question, Mr. Smith," Mandy said

crisply. "When people come to you and say they have been abducted, how do you know they are telling the truth?"

"We do not expect people to supply proof, if that's what you mean. But we know the truth when we hear it."

"I see. And what do you do for these people?" Mandy asked. "How do you help them?"

Mr. Smith frowned. "It's they who help, by coming forward. The more abductees who speak out, the more chance we have of being heard and believed. Only when the aliens are exposed will Earth be safe."

"I see." Mandy sat down.

Quentin leaned close. "No one can help you, Mandy," he whispered. "No one but me."

Mandy was sick of Quentin. A flare of anger burst in her head. She whipped around. "You —"

But the black-haired woman was looking at her with such sorrow, such pity, that Mandy's words died forgotten in her throat. She jumped from her chair.

"Luke," she cried. "I'm leaving."

Without waiting to see if he would come, she headed for the door. But she'd forgotten the skinheads.

They stood, shoulder to shoulder, jamming the door. They watched her with detached but avid interest.

Mandy noticed that one of them had an arm paler and thinner than his other arm. She flashed back to her mother's story about the abusive jerk whose broken arm had mended so miraculously. This had to be him.

For some reason this frightened her more than their obvious eagerness to have some fun with her.

Mandy stopped abruptly, facing them. Luke touched her arm and moved in front of her. Terror electrified her. Again she remembered seeing his head roll at her feet in the dust. A hallucination, but so real.

Before Mandy could stop Luke from putting himself in danger, the velvety voice spoke over her shoulder. "Play nice, boys. It's time to leave."

The dark-haired woman sailed implacably forward. She passed Luke and Mandy. Her deep-set eyes were focused on some distant point. Mandy watched in fascination.

The skinheads shifted uneasily. The human barrier rippled, swayed.

Mandy flinched as Quentin shoved past her, brushing her breast with his arm. She bit her lip to keep from crying out.

"Come on, guys," he said breezily.

The skinheads turned on their heels. They drained out of the doorway like water out of a funnel.

The woman's gait had never faltered. She missed treading on the last one's heel by a hair.

Mandy gulped down breaths of fresh air as she and Luke exited the building. Of course, they still had to make it out of the parking lot.

Ahead of them, the elegant woman slowed. "I am Cassandra," she said as Luke and Mandy drew even with her. There was banked fire in her dark eyes.

"Hi," Luke responded. "I'm —"

"I know who you are," she said, cutting him off. "Listen carefully. Time is short."

Beyond, Mandy caught a sharp movement. Quentin had seen them. He had his arm around that skinhead girl. He started across the parking lot toward them.

"Next time," Cassandra advised, her eyes flicking intently between Luke and Mandy, "pretend you are asleep. It is the only way to stay conscious. Keep your eyes closed and hold your breath for the first thirty seconds after you are lifted. Then breathe as evenly as you can. It is too late for me, but you can still be saved."

She looked over her shoulder at Quentin's approach. "DO NOT OPEN YOUR EYES UNTIL YOU ARE INSIDE THE SHIP!"

"What —"

The woman turned away. She began fumbling in her purse for something, in a hurry. Car keys appeared in her hand. And another Mars bar.

"Cass," Quentin called, "can I walk you to your car?"

The woman strode past Quentin without answering. She opened the door of the silvery sports car and tore the wrapper off the candy bar.

As she slid into the car, she stuffed the candy bar into her mouth. When she noticed Mandy staring, she rolled down the window. Her perfect mouth was smeared with chocolate.

"Isn't it wonderful," she said with a cackling laugh. "I can eat anything I want and never gain an ounce. HA HA HA HA!"

Still cackling at the top of her lungs, Cassandra threw the car into gear and zoomed off.

"Oh, gross," Luke said.

Mandy realized he was looking at Quentin.

Although Quentin's arm was around the skinhead girl, his eyes were fastened on Luke and Mandy. His long tongue was protruding from his mouth like a writhing snake.

When Quentin saw he had Mandy's attention, he whipped his tongue around behind the head of the skinhead girl. Delicately, he inserted the wiggly tip in her ear.

The girl inclined her head and giggled, her black-painted mouth opening like a gash in her face.

"Yes, Quentin, anything you say," she cried, although Quentin hadn't spoken.

Her throat closing, Mandy grabbed Luke's hand.

They turned and ran, Quentin's braying laughter echoing in their ears.

Chapter Twenty

"I told my parents I was sleeping at Sue Ellen's," Mandy said as she met Luke on the corner at the end of her street at nine-thirty that night.

She was wearing baggy coveralls and had her hair pulled back in a scrunchie. "So I don't know what I'm going to do all night."

"You can sleep on the couch in my basement," Luke said.

"Won't your parents mind?"

Luke shook his head. "I didn't even have to come up with a story for tonight. They're so worried about Jeff, they don't have any energy left over for me. He never even came home for dinner tonight."

Luke was pretty worried about Jeff himself. But he was even more angry. Teaming up with Quentin and throwing his weight around like a thug was about as low as Jeff could get, Luke figured.

They hefted their sleeping bags and headed for the power-line junction. The night was dark, clear, and mild. For a while they didn't speak, lost in their own thoughts and misgivings.

But as the pylons came in sight, Mandy started to wonder out loud about Cassandra. "Who do you suppose she is, Luke? Do you think she's crazy? How would she come to know Quentin?"

"I don't know," Luke replied. He couldn't tell Mandy that he thought the mysterious woman was an abductee who regretted joining the aliens. That would only set her off.

"I've got a theory," Mandy offered.

Luke grinned at her. "Now, why am I not surprised?"

Mandy made a face at him, and continued. "I think she's a mesmerist. A hypnotist."

Luke hadn't expected that. The background buzz of the power lines made it sound even more strange. "A hypnotist?"

Mandy's nervous eyes were fixed on the wires swaying overhead. "Let's set up first. I can't concentrate."

They stepped off the road, walked past the area where Mandy had put her dad's video camera, and entered the woods. Once they found enough of a clearing, they spread out their sleeping bags side by side.

"I can't see what this is going to accomplish," Mandy said. "But I think Cassandra was really trying to tell us something helpful."

Luke plopped down on his sleeping bag, resting his weight on his elbows. He looked at Mandy. "Hypnotism?" he prompted.

Mandy sat cross-legged on her sleeping bag. She pulled the scrunchie out of her hair and began to play with it absently. "Remember I told you Quentin has always seemed to have an uncanny ability to know what will hurt someone most?"

Luke nodded. He recalled Quentin telling their kindergarten teacher Luke was afraid to go to sleep because he still wet the bed and was afraid he would do it in school.

That had been Luke's secret fear, known to no one in the world but him. Quentin had done worse things since then, plenty worse, but that was the one that came first to mind.

"He killed my goldfish," Mandy continued, "and later my hamster died right after a visit from Quentin. But there was one thing nobody but me knew. My mom had promised I could have a puppy for Christmas if I proved I could take care of the fish and the rodent.

"He came up to me afterwards and said," —

Mandy pursed up her lips and did a passable imitation of Quentin's reedy, little-boy voice — "'Too bad you won't be getting a puppy. I wanted to see how it would get along with the Hughes' Rottweiler.'"

Luke sucked in his breath. "I had a puppy when I was seven. It escaped somehow and got into the Hughes' yard." He swallowed, thinking of the bloody, torn rag he had glimpsed before his father pulled him away. "I never wanted another dog after that."

"Oh, Luke."

They were silent for a few minutes, then Mandy sighed. "Quentin only lives a block from me," she said. "And closer to the power-line junction. I think he's been the one most affected by the electrical activity. His psychic power has been boosted."

Mandy dropped the scrunchie and turned to face Luke. He couldn't see her features clearly in the darkness, but he could still feel her intensity.

"In order to better focus that power, he went to a hypnotist. Cassandra. It's Quentin who's been projecting those nightmare visions on both of us." Mandy's hands were balled into fists. "Now she's caught on to what kind of monster he is and she's trying to stop him."

"Okay, Mandy." Luke sat up and tried to see her eyes. "But what does that have to do with all this?" He indicated the woods, the sleeping bags. "Why should we pretend to sleep but not sleep, keep our eyes closed, all of that?"

"Because Quentin works best on sleeping subjects," Mandy said. "If we're only pretending, we'll catch him at it. Then we can make all this stop."

Luke nodded slowly. He was thinking that last night they hadn't been asleep. At least not to begin with.

"If we're awake when the surge hits, he must project some sleep command," Mandy explained further, as if she too could read his mind. "So if we're pretending, he won't do that."

"And that stuff about the ship. 'Don't open your eyes until you're in the ship'? What does that mean?"

"It's a metaphor," Mandy insisted. She flopped down on her sleeping bag and put her arms behind her head. "And don't ask for what. I don't know. But I'm sure we're going to find out."

Luke lay down next to her. They both stared up at the stars.

"Think about it, Luke. Each time we've lost more than four hours. If Quentin can harness the electrical surge rather than become overloaded, then he had all that time to mess with our heads. But not this time."

Luke thought there were some holes in her

logic. But as she said, they would find out soon enough.

The power lines crackled loudly. They both stiffened.

"Relax," Luke whispered. "We're asleep, remember?"

They waited, tense, making an effort to look comatose. Luke didn't see how it could possibly work. His heart was loud in his ears.

The lines sputtered and crackled and sparked. But nothing happened. After a while Luke felt his eyelids actually growing heavy.

"Mandy," he said abruptly, jerking his eyes open.

"Mmm? Oh! I was almost asleep."

"Me, too. We need to keep talking." Naturally he couldn't think of a single thing to say.

"Isn't the sky beautiful," Mandy said. "I wish I had brought my telescope. Have you ever looked at the planets through a telescope?"

Luke had to admit he hadn't.

"It's so great," Mandy enthused. "Sometimes you can even see the moons around Jupiter."

Mandy talked about how she could get lost in the sky through her telescope and he told her he felt the same about sports.

The power lines sputtered, sending out a shower of sparks. Luke and Mandy both stiffened and shut their eyes. But again, nothing happened.

They talked and talked for what seemed like hours. Every once in a while, the high-tension wires would make them jump. But it was never anything. Still, Luke thought, it wasn't a total waste of time. Who would ever have thought it could be so interesting talking to a girl?

"Nothing's going to happen tonight," Mandy said after a while. "We should go."

Luke agreed, but they lay there a little longer, watching the sky, being quiet together.

He was about to get up when the power lines gave off a loud crackle and an angry sputter of sparks. There was a brilliant flash of light. Different from before.

"This is it!" Luke whispered excitedly. "Close your eyes. Remember to hold your breath."

No answer.

"Mandy!" he hissed urgently.

She didn't stir. Mandy was really asleep!

Panicked, he started to reach over and shake her. But another flash of light froze him.

He shut his eyes as the sky began to blank out. A cold wind blew across his sleeping bag and snatched at his breath. The air went dead still and the weird electronic hum invaded his body.

His bones were vibrating. Somehow he forced himself to keep his eyes closed. His breathing was ragged. It took all his willpower to slow his heaving lungs. He felt like he was drowning.

All at once his body began to lift into the air. Every muscle tensed to fight. Gritting his teeth, he concentrated on going limp, fighting all his human instincts. His heart battered at his rib cage.

Luke held his breath. Not an instant too soon, he realized, as a light mist fell on his face. He counted the seconds, forcing himself to go slow.

And then, just when he thought enough time had passed to take a breath, a wad of slime slapped down over his head.

The cold, gummy substance slicked itself to his face. It flowed over his eyes, nose, mouth. He felt it slide down, molding his arms to his sides, wrapping his legs, congealing around his body.

It hardened instantly. His body was rigid. He felt like a mummy in a tight coffin.

Claustrophobic panic seized him. He couldn't breathe. His mind exploded with terror. Every cell in his body wanted to thrash for freedom.

Luke fought for calm. He kept repeating in his head, "They must think I'm asleep, they must think I'm asleep." Though his muscles twitched beneath his skin, he didn't move.

And then the sky fell on him. His body felt compressed to a pancake from the force of acceleration. As his stomach squeezed against his backbone, he began to panic again.

He was hurtling through space and he couldn't see, couldn't hear. How much force could a human body take before his bones snapped and his innards ruptured?

Luke was about to succumb to his mindless panic when his speed slowed.

His body seemed to drop suddenly. He heard a click and felt a change of pressure. His ears popped.

His motion stopped abruptly and he heard the noise of machinery.

He was inside the alien spaceship.

Chapter Twenty-one

Luke lay perfectly still. He kept his eyes shut, but strained his ears for some sign of what was happening. All he could hear was the hum of machinery. And an odd sucking sound.

Phwup. Phphwuup!

Cautiously, Luke opened his eyes. He didn't expect to be able to see. He was still cocooned in the alien carapace.

But light shone into his eyes. Too bright. Then a shadow passed over his face and he could focus.

It took him a second to realize what was happening. A giant disk was descending right over his face. It grew larger, filling his vision.

It was right on top of him. About to crush his head.

Without thinking, Luke flinched away.

His head turned. His body followed. He was rolling.

Panic gripped Luke like a vise. He braced himself to fall, tensed for the shout of discovery that would come any second.

But there was no shout. He came to rest in weightlessness. There was nothing under him. Luke twisted to look. His whole body turned.

The floor was there. Below him. About four feet. There was nothing between it and his floating body.

Phwup. Phphwuup!

Luke's pulse jumped. He jerked to look for the noise and tumbled wildly in midair. The room whirled. What little he could see as he spun filled him with increasing horror.

The spinning slowed, stopped. Carefully, Luke turned his head toward the sucking noise. He saw himself. Luke. Lying motionless on a gurney.

A large machine was suctioning the transport carapace off him. Large transparent sheets disappeared into a thick hose. It was the same substance as the piece he had found in the woods.

Slowly Luke looked down to see the lower half of his floating, conscious self. Arms, legs, torso, all there. But transparent, like a ghost.

He felt queasy, but no longer panicked. Frightened, maybe, but not terrified. It was a bit like it had been in the vision this morning when he saw himself and then Mandy.

Mandy. Slowly getting the feel of his non-body, Luke turned, looking for her. She was on another gurney a few feet away. A second machine was sucking the carapace off her. Her eyes were closed.

There was no one else around. Tentatively, Luke tried a small kick, figuring that floating would be a lot like swimming. Slowly, he moved toward Mandy. Stopping was more of a problem. But he was able pretty much to use the air in here like he would water.

He floated close to her ear. "Mandy. Can you hear me? Mandy?"

There was no response. He hadn't expected any.

He looked around more closely. He and Mandy were in a room that looked like an operating theater. Unknown equipment surrounded both gurneys. All of it looked clean, polished, and clinical.

There weren't any windows. One wall curved outward. The floor was level, the other three walls vertical. The surfaces were a luminous gray, almost silver. Metallic-looking.

Against one wall was a bank of strange-looking computers, like nothing ever seen on Earth. Their screens were blank.

There was a noise somewhere outside the room. It was a low, buzzy, chuffing sound. Nothing Luke had ever heard before.

But it worried him. He had to try and wake Mandy. Maybe they could find their way out of here before the — the — *owners* came.

"Mandy. Wake up!" Luke put his mouth right up to her ear. "Mandy," he called as loud as he dared.

She was out cold. The chuffing noise was coming closer.

His pulse ratcheted up to jet speed. He reached out to grab Mandy's shoulder and shake her. His hand passed right through her.

He stared in shock at his transparent hand. His mind went momentarily blank.

Snick! A section of the wall slid smoothly open. Luke froze as three of them came in.

The creatures from his nightmares.

They had enormous bulbous heads. Their bodies were slender and sexless under silvery, translucent garments. The skin he could see was skim-milk white, as if these creatures had never been touched by sunlight.

But it was their eyes that chilled him most of all.

Almost half their faces were taken up by bulging insectoid eyes. The room's even lighting was reflected mirrorlike off of them. Luke couldn't tell which way they were looking.

But he knew the instant he moved, they would see him. And if they saw him, he had no chance of getting out alive.

At the moment, they were engaged in some spirited discussion. The buzzy chuffing sound came from small, almost lipless mouths. From the way their heads jerked and the sharp movements of their arms, it looked to Luke like they were disagreeing about something.

When they moved — quick movements especially — the part of them in motion seemed to disappear briefly. As if they were barely visible in the human spectrum.

Luke remembered the creature he had chased in the woods. All he'd been able to see of it was a shimmer in the air. What a talent!

The trio of aliens moved toward Luke's own motionless body. Luke took the chance to dive under Mandy's gurney. It wasn't a good hiding place. They would see him when they came to examine Mandy.

Meanwhile, he couldn't see a thing.

He raised his head to see where they were. He also tried to find a better hiding place. At the exact moment his eyes cleared the gurney, one of the beings turned around. Reflected light flashed off its eyes into Luke's.

It had seen him. Luke ducked his head. Three pairs of legs winked in and out of sight as they scissored his way. He was caught.

He couldn't fight. Where could he run to? The ship must be full of them.

The blur of motion was almost on him. Luke

looked up. If his hand could pass through Mandy, chances were his body could pass through the ceiling.

But the prospect terrified him. He knew he had to try to escape, but his mind was full of frantic what-ifs.

What if he was separated from his body forever? What if he found himself in space and was instantly annihilated?

They were almost on him. Luke launched himself into the air.

Light blinded him.

One of the aliens had looked right at him.

Chapter Twenty-two

Luke bounced, careening right off the ceiling.

His heart stopped dead. They had him now.

He twisted, and aimed for the open door. At least he wouldn't make it easy for them.

Diving frantically for the door, Luke miscalculated. His head smacked the side before he could jerk away.

There was no pain. He was in a long gently curved hallway. Somehow his head had passed through the door frame. But he could not pass through the ceiling even though it all seemed made of the same gray metal.

There was no time to wonder about it. He fled, kicking like a swimmer. But he could see no way out, no spot to hide.

The hall was featureless.

Luke ran his hand along the wall as he went,

pressing. He could feel the surface. It was cool and there seemed to be a faint vibration.

He risked a glance backwards. No aliens yet. Unless they were coming so fast he couldn't see them.

Suddenly his arm plunged through the wall. His head and shoulders followed before he could reverse. Panicked, he scrambled to throw himself back into the hall.

But the room was empty.

Instantly, excitement gripped him.

Two high-backed molded seats faced a darkened expanse — a windshield. In front of each seat was a dizzying array of gauges and dials and computer keyboards molded for hands that were not human.

He was in the pilot's command module.

Strange-looking squiggles labeled many of the dials. Naturally none of it meant anything to Luke. Gingerly, he pressed a large black button. His finger passed right through.

Disappointed, he tried a few more keys, with the same result.

This was getting him nowhere. But still, he hadn't been caught. Maybe they didn't care if his useless ghost wandered the ship.

Cautiously, Luke stuck his head back into the hallway. It was empty. Either nothing was after him or they had gone past. Slipping back into the hall, he thought he should explore as much of the ship as he could.

If he ever got out, he could warn someone.

He floated farther down the passage, running his hand along the wall, pressing lightly. He didn't want to fall into some room without warning again.

And then — *snick*. The wall slid open and an alien stepped out right in front of him. Merely a foot away.

Luke grabbed the wall, scrambling to turn. It was like trying to make sudden moves underwater.

The alien turned toward him. Its huge eyes looked directly at him. And then it walked right through him.

Luke pressed himself against the wall, shuddering. Slowly his rush of adrenaline subsided. It hadn't seen him. It hadn't known he was there at all. As far as the aliens were concerned, he was invisible.

Instantly he felt charged. But undecided. Should he go back? Should he see what was happening to him and Mandy? Or should he explore the ship further?

The thought of going back to the examining room filled him with dread. He was helpless to stop them.

Luke turned the other way. Maybe he could

find a way out. A way to stop these creatures permanently.

He felt for the doorway the alien had come though and slipped inside. For a minute he couldn't breathe.

The room was filled with aliens.

Luke reminded himself they couldn't see him. But he still felt horribly exposed as he floated to the ceiling. From there he had a view of the whole room.

Aliens in small groups stood at high counters or sat at small tables. They were eating. This was the cafeteria.

The aliens' eyes were dulled with absorption. Their plates of food were reflected darkly in the opaque facets of their eyes. All of them seemed to be eating the same thing. Some kind of brown mass.

Luke wanted to heave. There were things moving on the plates. As Luke swooped closer, he saw something small scurry off onto a table.

An alien, its arm a blur, speared the small creature with a pointed silver stick. It stuck the wiggling thing in its mouth.

Luke turned away, sickened. He found himself facing a wall stacked with glass boxes. Inside, fat black rats could barely turn around. Other boxes contained swarms of huge, sluggish cockroaches.

Dinner.

He'd seen enough. But as he headed back toward the door, it opened. Voices. Luke felt ice in his veins. One of the voices was unmistakably human — and familiar.

"Don't rush it, dude, I'm hungry. They're not going anywhere." Quentin entered. Looking around, his own eyes glittered more than the giant orbs of the aliens. "Just a snack."

Luke pressed against the wall. There was nowhere to hide. He tried to shrink himself very small. For some reason, the thought of Quentin spying him was even scarier than being caught by the aliens.

But Quentin looked right through Luke. He walked over to one of the glass boxes and pulled out a rat. The alien accompanying him said something in its chittering buzz.

Quentin turned on him, scowling. He held up the wiggling rat. "Monotonous? Are you complaining? I'll have you know many earthlings would consider such food a delicacy. Pure protein."

Savagely, Quentin bared his strong, white teeth and in one bite decapitated the rat. He threw his head back and let blood spurt into his open mouth.

"Of course," he said, licking blood off his lips, "you can always go out and get your own food. See if you can find any before you suffocate from oxygen deprivation."

Quentin grinned and breathed deep. "I love the energy high I get in this place. The extra oxygen always makes me feel so jaunty and carefree."

He cast the body of the rat aside and turned his attention to its head. He thrust out his tongue. As Luke watched, the tongue elongated. Quentin probed the skull of the rat with the slender tip, finally securing a small, glistening morsel.

"The brains are always the best part," he said, smacking his lips. "Now, let's go inspect the new recruits."

Quentin headed for the door, trailed by the alien. At the door, Quentin stopped.

"Don't you forget," he said flatly, warning the alien.

He looked up and took in the whole room with the jut of his chin. He raised his voice. "Don't any of you dyzychs forget," he shouted in a tone as cold as death itself. "You need me more than I need you."

Luke knew he had to follow them. But he felt he needed a minute to recoup. He floated near the ceiling, trying to calm himself. Icy jitters raced up and down his spine.

He couldn't help noticing many of the aliens had stopped eating. Some had pushed away half-finished plates. Maybe they were just bored with rat — or else Quentin had taken away their appetites.

Luke took in a deep breath . . .

. . . and was suddenly yanked back through the closed door. The passageway blurred past him.

His arms and legs flailed in panic.

They'd found him out!

Chapter Twenty-three

Mandy jerked awake and sat up in the sleeping bag, instantly panicked.

"Luke, wake up! Luke!" She looked at her watch but it was too dark to see. "I can't believe we fell asleep. At least nothing happened."

Luke groaned. "We're back," he said.

The hair on the back of Mandy's neck prickled. Luke sounded surprised, relieved.

"It must be that our spirits get pulled back inside when they send us back," Luke continued.

"What are you talking about?" Mandy asked. "What time is it?"

"It's two o'clock in the morning, Mandy, but we weren't sleeping. We were abducted," Luke explained patiently. "It happened just like Cassandra said it would. I could see and hear everything, but the aliens had no idea. I'm sorry, I couldn't wake you in time."

Mandy couldn't believe her ears. She felt hollow inside. "Aliens? Luke, are you listening to yourself? Look at us — we're still in our sleeping bags. Nothing happened. You had a nightmare."

"It wasn't a dream or a hallucination." Luke spilled it all out, every outlandish detail. To Mandy, he seemed like a born-again zombie.

Mandy's mind was reeling. Luke's mind had snapped. She was the only one still sane.

Her mind groped for inconsistencies, the types of things that seemed real only in dreams. She had to make Luke see. Otherwise, she would be all alone again.

"If all these, um, aliens make is a buzzy noise, how could Quentin communicate with them?" Mandy asked. "Not to mention, how did he ever hook up with them in the first place? What would they need with a human?"

Luke shook his head. "I don't know, but I suppose it probably has to do with what you were saying earlier. Quentin's psychic powers."

Mandy's spirits plummeted further. She had planted this awful seed herself.

Suddenly, Luke looked at her, his eyes wide and horrified. "Mandy, I just had a terrible thought. The way Quentin talked to them.

Swaggering. As if he was in charge. What if the aliens are here *because* of him? Because they need him?"

"Oh, please, Luke. Why would they need a sociopathic creep like Quentin?"

"Maybe to herd in the human subjects for their experiments. People like us."

Suddenly Mandy had an idea of her own. She couldn't wait to get home.

"Home? But your parents think you're at Sue Ellen's," Luke argued. "You can't go home."

Mandy shrugged impatiently. She rolled up her sleeping bag and slung it over her shoulder. "I have to. Before it gets light. My parents will be asleep and I can get in through the basement. I'll tell them I couldn't sleep and came home at dawn."

"But why?" Luke asked. "What's the rush?"

She was touched that he didn't want her to go. "You think you were whisked to a spaceship, right?"

"*We*," Luke told her. "We *both* were."

"Whatever. It can't be far away. I know the sky around here like the back of my hand," Mandy said. "If there's a spaceship out there, I'll find it."

Luke suddenly shared her enthusiasm. They grabbed their gear and headed for the road. The wires buzzed softly, as if even they were sleeping.

"Call me when you find it," Luke said. "Then we can figure out what to do next."

"Sure." Mandy was hoping that with first light, Luke would come to his senses. Even the most vivid dreams dissolved when the sun shone on them. Usually.

She had no trouble getting back into the house, and got the telescope up onto the roof without too much noise. Because she didn't expect to find anything, she was even more careful than she ordinarily would be.

Mandy played her telescope over every inch of sky. And then she did it again. And again. Until the sun came up and the stars disappeared.

She called Luke. "You said it took only a few minutes to reach the ship," she reminded him. "Then where is it? All the stars and planets are in place. There's nothing up there that shouldn't be. No UFOs."

She tried to keep any hint of smugness out of her voice.

But Luke didn't seem disappointed. Quite the opposite.

"Then it's on the ground," he said excitedly. "That means we can find it. Something that big can't be easy to hide. Mandy, it's probably near where I chased the alien and got zapped in the woods. Quentin said they can't go far in our atmosphere. Not enough oxygen. They can't leave the ship for long, which is why they need Quentin."

Mandy felt exhausted. She craved sleep. But she couldn't let Luke go alone.

She argued with herself. There was nothing to find, so why not let him go? Quentin and his merry band of skinhead thugs, that's why. Quentin might not be a wanna-be alien, but there *was* something evil going on with him.

Mandy had no doubt it was dangerous. In the real world.

She talked Luke into letting her get a couple hours sleep. They met at the high-tension junction just after lunch.

It was immediately obvious that the daylight hadn't diminished Luke's belief in alien abduction one bit. "We should split up for efficiency," he said.

"No way," Mandy balked. She was not tramping around in the woods by herself. "What if something happened to one of us?"

Luke didn't seem too disappointed. But it was a wasted afternoon. No aliens, no danger, just a lot of scratchy bushes.

Mandy got home exhausted. She was in no mood to have Luke call to remind her not to sleep.

"Drink plenty of coffee," he instructed. "Go to bed before ten, but *don't* fall asleep. Okay? Together we'll find a way out of this."

It was his last sentence that made her go along.

She drank three cups of coffee and still felt drowsy. So she drank a fourth. All the caffeine seemed to kick in about ten minutes later.

Nerves jangling, she put on her only pair of pajamas. If the power surge scrambled her brain, she might sleepwalk again. And if Quentin was waiting, she wanted to be wearing more than a T-shirt and panties.

At the mere thought of his name, a sudden image hit Mandy like a fist. Quentin, snaky tongue whiplashing, coming for her. Another figure in the background, eyes like a giant fly's.

The hallucination was gone in a second, but Mandy sat down on the edge of her bed, shaking. She wished she was with Luke. She should have found some way they could spend the night together again.

She got up. It was nine-thirty. She grabbed her desk chair and wedged the top of it under her doorknob. That might not stop her from sleepwalking, but maybe the noise would wake her parents.

Getting into bed, she realized she couldn't even read. But what was stopping her? She wouldn't be sleeping. And Luke wouldn't know she hadn't actually pretended to sleep.

But maybe Quentin would.

Mandy turned out the light. Immediately,

images floated up in the darkness. Creatures with huge, cold eyes and pale, boneless limbs. Strange, gleaming instruments.

And Quentin, lifting her shirt with his serpentine tongue.

Mandy jerked out her arm to turn on the light.

But there already was light. Her room was filling with it.

Mandy's arm fell back on the bed. The light was cool, like gray dawn. Her room was empty.

Brighter light flashed outside her window. Mandy shut her eyes. Suddenly terrified, she stopped breathing.

In her mind, she heard Cassandra. "Hold your breath. Keep your eyes closed."

Her body was rigid. Mandy tried to relax her muscles.

This wasn't really happening. Just another horrible hallucination. In a few seconds she was going to turn on her lamp.

Then the covers slid off. Mandy stifled a scream.

She felt her body lift off the bed.

Chapter Twenty-four

This wasn't happening.

Nevertheless, Mandy continued to hold her breath when she felt the mist hit her face. She was braced for the cold fall of thick liquid that Luke had described. It molded her arms to her sides.

She didn't panic when the shell hardened, encasing her body. Luke had prepared her well. Too well. It was his hallucination she was having. Somehow she was dreaming his dream.

Oh, well. Her own nightmare might have been worse.

An abrupt sensation of acceleration cut off her thoughts. Her stomach pressed sickeningly against her backbone as she was hurled through space.

But the unpleasant sensation was brief, as Luke had promised. Then she was inside. Mandy wondered: Would Luke be here, too?

Mandy hoped she wouldn't have to suffer through this experience on her own.

"Mandy," Luke's voice called anxiously. "Are you awake?"

Mandy opened her eyes and there he was, hovering. Beyond him — no, *through* him — she could see his body, and the large machine removing his carapace.

"I'm awake," Mandy whispered. Experimentally, she tried rolling. There was the slightest tug of resistance, and then she was free and weightless.

She kind of liked it.

Mandy smiled at Luke. She kicked to float up beside him and overshot, knocking her head on the ceiling. She was surprised to discover it didn't hurt.

Luke rose, still looking anxious.

"I've read about astral projections," Mandy said. "I always wondered how it would feel. I suppose this is it."

"Astral projection?" Luke wrinkled his nose. "Isn't that some New Age thing?"

Mandy shrugged. "I guess. Although it's nothing new. Some people claim their astral selves leave their bodies and travel during sleep. I always thought it sounded cool. Sleep is such a waste of time."

She looked around. "This really is clinical-looking. And so gray. Even the light is dim and silvery. There's no color at all. Usually I dream in vivid color."

"Dream? I wondered why you seem so calm about all this," Luke said, shaking his head. "Mandy, this is not a dream."

"Says you. Come on, let's go find some aliens." Mandy twisted around, spinning in the air. "Where's the door?"

Luke led the way. He took her first to the control room, but naturally the symbols meant no more to her than they had to him.

She didn't see her first alien until they reached the "roachateria," as Luke dubbed it. A wave of revulsion washed over her. It was a visceral feeling, twisting her guts.

It was the aliens' eyes that bothered her, even more than their revolting eating habits. Obviously the creatures were intelligent, but their huge eyes were as empty as any insect's.

"That was as far as I got last night," Luke said as they left. "From here on, everything is new to both of us."

A hatch opened in the wall, spilling silvery light over the passageway. An alien came out and turned down the hall away from Luke and Mandy, leaving the door open.

Mandy was surprised to notice how gracefully the alien creature moved. Even though its limbs looked unnaturally slender under the oversize head, the creature seemed almost to glide, its motion was so smooth.

With a kick, Mandy followed Luke toward the open hatchway. She found that she liked astral flying. It was, as Luke had said, a bit like swimming.

Except air didn't have the resistance of water. As usual, she overflew her target and had to come back.

"It's another examining room. A laboratory," Luke told her. "There's nobody here."

"It looks like they're prepping it," Mandy said, eyeing the instruments positioned around an empty space. Computers were humming, although the screens were blank.

Mandy felt a prickle of unease. She had to remind herself it was only a dream. "I wonder if it's for us," she said.

"There isn't room for both of us," Luke pointed out.

As he spoke, they heard a trundling sound in the passageway. It was accompanied by a chittering noise — like grasshoppers crawling over one another.

Goose bumps rose on Mandy's astral flesh. "What's that awful noise?"

"The buzzing sound? That's how they talk. The aliens."

"It vibrates inside me," Mandy complained.

"Like insect legs scraping the inside of my scalp."

"Really? It doesn't have that effect on me," Luke said.

The sound grew louder. Mandy shuddered and rose to a corner of the ceiling. She had to fight the urge to flee.

Suddenly, the aliens were in the room. They wheeled a gurney into place. She couldn't see who it was; the aliens blocked her view.

"Mrs. Grundy!" Luke exclaimed in surprise.

"What?" Mandy swooped down. Too fast. Unable to stop, she plunged right through an alien's head. Her wheeling arms churned the body on the gurney before she was able to slip sideways.

Although she felt no flesh and the aliens gave no indication of sensing anything unusual, the experience nauseated her. She reached for Luke to steady herself, but her hand passed through him. She cartwheeled once more before coming to a shaky stop.

"Make small movements," Luke said, but he seemed hardly conscious of her distress. His attention was focused on the aliens.

Mandy pulled up beside him. Mrs. Grundy was unconscious. She was dressed in an old cotton nightgown, with a rip in one short sleeve. Clearly, she had not been expecting company.

The aliens were attaching wires to the old

lady's head. The wires were tipped with small needles, like tacks, which the creatures pressed into her scalp.

Mandy noticed that the aliens' arms seemed boneless, bending in odd, fluid ways. They also seemed to elongate and shorten at will. It reminded her of something. She wasn't sure what.

"What could they want with her?" Mandy asked in a small voice. She felt it was her fault the old librarian was here in her nightmare.

Luke and Mandy both stiffened at the sound of approaching footsteps in the hall. The aliens didn't make footstep sounds.

"Quentin," breathed Luke.

"Ah, you've started," Quentin said, entering. He rubbed his hands together happily. "Is she conscious?"

He was wearing a bright-red T-shirt. With a start, Mandy realized it was the first color she had seen in the ship. Her heart lurched. Quentin seemed so horribly real.

The aliens chittered.

"Yes, she's old." Quentin grinned at the aliens. "Didn't I tell you? No?"

When the aliens raised their heads, Mandy saw their eyes no longer had that empty look. A shiver of fright ran through her.

The eyes glittered from multiple facets. It was impossible to see into them, impossible even to look right at them. Blinding reflections of light refracted in all directions. They were not made for the human way of seeing.

Quentin seemed unaffected. "Well, I wanted her and that's that. She was very good to me when I was little. In ways other humans would never understand. You might say she presided over my education. Besides"— Quentin shrugged, turning to the computer monitors — "she's dying of cancer."

He touched a button and the monitors lit up. One screen showed a human brain. The others were still blank.

Quentin pressed a button. Light pulsed in the pictured brain. Mrs. Grundy jerked and thrashed. "Oops," Quentin laughed. "Wrong button."

He pressed another and the old lady's parched lips relaxed into a crooked smile. Drool ran from the corner of her mouth. "Much better."

Leaving the monitors, Quentin walked over to the gurney. The dyzychs made way for him.

"If this works out, I'd like to do the recruits next. You'll need to hurry. I sense that time is short. In fact, I'll give the order now. No need to wait." Quentin licked his lips. "Full treatment for the female, I think."

Mandy jumped with alarm.

"No," Quentin said sharply. "Not that one.

Not Mandy. The new one. I have special plans for Mandy." His tongue wiggled suggestively.

With a shudder, Mandy realized what the sinewy alien arms had reminded her of. They were like Quentin's tongue.

"She's mine and you are not to mess with her," Quentin ordered. His tone was hard but also gruff with desire. "My plans require her to be in a fully human context."

Mandy was frozen with horror.

"Come on, Mandy," Luke urged, clearly disturbed. "Let's get out of here. We can't help. And we need to explore the ship, to see if we can figure out where it is."

"I need this to be over," Mandy said weakly. None of her hallucinations, however horrible, had lasted as long as this one.

Quentin turned toward the door, his eyes blazing with evil joy. It radiated from him in waves that washed over Mandy's astral form, leaving her gasping for air. She felt unclean.

Quentin's tongue whipped back and forth. Before Mandy could move, it had slashed through her.

She felt a stabbing pain, like an icicle through her heart.

"I have to wake up," she cried.

But it wasn't over yet.

Chapter Twenty-five

Luke hated feeling so helpless.

He couldn't even touch Mandy to comfort her. Or punch out that rat-eating creep Quentin.

Mandy leaned against the wall in the passageway, trembling uncontrollably.

"When we get out of here, we'll go after him," Luke told her. He imagined his flesh-and-blood fists smashing into that smug face. "We'll stop him, Mandy."

But even as he spoke, he remembered how Quentin had immobilized him. More than once.

Mandy had told him about the head-severing incident. She had been trying to convince him of Quentin's psychic power to project hallucinations.

Instead Luke remembered how his neck had mysteriously hurt. And he was convinced that Quentin could have killed him on the spot, if he'd wanted to. And Luke wouldn't even have known it.

"I'm all right," Mandy said finally. "I suppose, if I can't wake up, we might as well explore. Anywhere where Quentin isn't."

Luke was glad to get away from the sound of alien needles puncturing the old librarian's body. Even in the passageway, the soft fleshy sound had seemed louder than the buzzy gabble of the dyzychs.

Luke and Mandy moved deeper into the ship. The hall continued to curve. Luke realized it would form a perfect circle eventually. The ship really *was* a flying saucer. Somehow the movies and books had gotten that part right.

Luke pressed the inner wall, looking for doors. With a falling plunge he would never get used to, he found one.

It was a large chamber, unlit and empty. Coffin-size tubes of some clear substance were stacked in rows, floor to ceiling.

"Sleeping places?" Luke conjectured. "But so many. Could there be this many dyzychs on this ship?"

"Everything's so gloomy," Mandy said. "I feel like all this gray is pressing on me."

"I suppose they don't see color," Luke said, flitting around one of the chambers. A hose ran from each capsule to an inside wall. "Extra oxygen when they're sleeping, I'll bet."

Mandy nodded mechanically. That worried Luke. She wasn't going to take any of this seriously if she kept thinking it was all in her head. And he needed her to take it *very* seriously.

Luke had a feeling something very bad was going to happen if they didn't stop it. If only he knew what "it" was.

At the sound of dyzychs passing by in the hallway, Luke and Mandy went out.

The aliens were moving quickly and waving their elastic arms. Their forms shimmered in and out of visibility.

"Something's up," Mandy said apprehensively.

A hatch door opened on the outside of the ring. The aliens went through it.

"Another examination-operation chamber." Luke sounded disappointed.

The room was large, partitioned into ten curtained cubicles. Wires and tubes snaked down into each cubicle from machines positioned overhead.

The wall beside the entrance was filled with monitors, gauges, and dials. Dyzychs moved between them, pressing buttons and adjusting dials intently.

"This place seems to be nothing but a flying laboratory," Mandy said. "Assuming it *does* fly."

She frowned thoughtfully. Then shook her head impatiently. "I'm not going to start analyzing my dreams while I'm still having them."

Luke didn't see any dyzych movement behind the thin silvery-white curtains. "I guess we'll have to look," he said reluctantly.

They heard a liquidy sucking noise from behind the curtain. Luke wanted to turn and flee. His breath was shallow. Then there was a loud crack, like a dry stick snapped in half.

He and Mandy both jumped. Without speaking, they moved as if drawn, through the curtain.

"Oh my god," Mandy moaned.

Luke felt his throat close.

On the gurney before them lay one of the skinheads. The top of his skull was missing. The gray folds of his brain glistened and quivered in the cool air.

Metal probes attached to thin electrical wires protruded from the exposed tissue.

Mandy gestured faintly at a table beside the gurney. A shiver climbed up the back of Luke's neck. The missing skull-half sat rocking in a white metal bowl.

On the flap of skin at the front, Luke read H-A-T-E.

"Whatever I wished on him, it wasn't *this*," Luke muttered.

Below the eyebrows, the skinhead's face was intact. The eyes were mercifully closed. His expression was blank.

The sucking noise began again, making Luke and Mandy jump. Luke had been so horribly fascinated by the naked brain, he hadn't noticed the two large tubes — hoses really — protruding from each shoulder.

The skinhead's left arm jerked spasmodically. Something lumpy slipped up the tube from inside the body.

"Luke, look," Mandy cried in a strangled voice.

At the head of the gurney was a small screen. It monitored the work of the tubes.

SNAP!

The right arm jerked and bent at an impossible angle.

"They're breaking his bones and vacuuming them out," Luke said, feeling a kind of awe at something so beyond his worst imaginings.

"Luke, we have to go and see what they're doing to *our* bodies," Mandy said urgently. "Now."

Luke shook his head, biting his lip. "Not yet," he told her. His mind felt thick. As if it finally was going into terminal overload.

"There are ten cubicles here." He forced the words out, groping for each one. "I have to check and see if my brother is in one of them."

If there had been blood in Mandy's face it would have drained. Her blue eyes darkened to the color of the deepest ocean depths. "I'll go with you," she said.

Together they moved through the curtain into the next cubicle, then the next and the next. In each of the next eight they found a skinhead boy, skull removed, arm bones fractured and suctioned away.

None of the boys was Jeff.

The last cubicle was different. Luke thought he was prepared for every horror. He wasn't.

There was a girl on the gurney.

Luke heard Mandy's sharp intake of breath. "I know her."

Luke's heart was fluttering weakly in his chest. He couldn't seem to get a breath.

"How can you tell?" he asked, gulping air. "She has no face."

As with the others, the top of the girl's head had been removed. In her case, the skin of her face had also been peeled away. It lay folded under her skull in a bowl.

There were empty holes where her eyes had been. A jellylike substance glistened in the recesses. Luke didn't see the girl's eyes in the bowl or anywhere.

Mandy pointed with a shaking finger. "The tattoo on her hand," she said. "She was with Quentin at that meeting."

The tattoo spelled LOVE. With no bones in her hand, the letters were crooked and collapsed. Her arms, too, were entirely boneless. The skin lay loose over flaccid, twitching muscles.

Suddenly it seemed vitally urgent to Luke that he and Mandy reconnect with their own bodies.

Luke heard Quentin's voice while they were speeding back along the corridor.

"You don't have to understand my reasons," Quentin was saying heatedly. "Just do it."

Do what? Luke put on a burst of speed.

As he and Mandy approached the open hatchway, he could see their bodies lying comatose, just as they had left them. Quentin was standing in the midst of a trio of buzzing and chittering dyzychs.

Then a second human voice spoke. "I think they're concerned about all those bones." The tone was detached, the voice deep and silky.

Luke's and Mandy's eyes met in surprise. Cassandra.

This astral stuff had been her suggestion. Would she be able to see them? Luke decided he was beyond caring. He shot through the open hatch without hesitating.

Cassandra was seated on a high stool in front of the computer equipment. Her eyes were on the monitors. She was wearing a dyzych garment. Its shimmery, revealing folds fell in a flattering drape around her.

"They've never operated in a body with rigid bones," she said languidly. "They're worried they might break some. Bend them the wrong way."

"So what?" Quentin shrugged. "I don't care about the bones. If they break" — his eyes shone briefly at the prospect — "you can fix them. Or remove them."

"It's not the subjects themselves they are worried about," Cassandra informed him, reaching to adjust a dial. Her arm did not bend at an angle. It curved. Luke felt a little sick.

The heart on the monitor in front of her pulsed harder. Luke somehow knew it was his own heart.

"The dyzychs are afraid of pain," said Cassandra. "They don't want to experience any, even secondhand."

Quentin exploded. "I've done plenty for you. Now you can do this for me. I want them fully human and fully aware." He paused. When he spoke again, his voice was flat.

"There isn't much time. The Others will be here soon. I can sense it. Thanks to me, the plan is going forward smoothly. We will have all the soldiers you need. But these two are mine. Now, *do it*."

The dyzychs separated. Two went to Mandy and Luke. They each selected one of the tubular silver tools. They removed the long needles and refitted the tool with shorter, blunter ones.

The two aliens moved in unison, as if performing a macabre dance. With their lethal-looking instruments ready, they turned together and looked at their third companion. Their eyes, cold as diamonds, glittered with reflected light.

The third dyzych had joined Cassandra at the computer bank. It now pressed a key and two more monitors lit up.

Each screen showed the inside of a human head. Luke's chest constricted. There was no doubt about whose skulls those were.

The alien's supple fingers danced over the keyboard. A midsection of Mandy's brain lit up. Then the same thing happened to Luke's brain.

The creature's bulbous head nodded once and the other two bent over their comatose prisoners. They fitted the instruments to Luke's and Mandy's temples.

A jolt of icy terror raced through Luke. Before he could react, a high-pitched whine vibrated the air with a loud drilling sound.

Mandy shrieked and dove for her body.

The stench of burning bone filled the room.

Chapter Twenty-six

Mandy's eyes snapped open. She was hyperventilating, her heart pounding like a jackhammer.

It was pitch-black, but she knew she was in her own room, in her own bed.

Bolting upright, she checked out her alarm clock. Three A.M. Longer this time. She snapped on the light. The chair was still hooked under the doorknob.

A thought passed through her mind — what difference did it make if the chair was in place? She had gone out the window. Or had she?

Mandy switched off the light. She didn't want her mom or dad seeing it and coming in, all concerned. She didn't want to see anyone until she had her head on straight again.

A dream. A horrible nightmare. She'd never had such a vivid nightmare before. It seemed she could still remember every awful second of the whole five hours.

Sweat trickled into her eyes and stung. She wiped it away and took a deep breath. These electrical surges were taking too great a toll. Any more of this and she'd have to fear for her sanity.

There were stories, lots of them, about people who had been normal happy children and then lost their minds completely as teenagers. They had to be locked away, screaming about demons and creatures coming to get them.

A cold feeling lodged in Mandy's chest as she imagined a lifetime of Quentin hallucinations, getting progressively more threatening and perverse. She'd rather die.

But she didn't have to. An idea burst in her head like a fireworks finale. All she had to do was leave Greenfield until the power surges were over. She should have thought of that before.

Suddenly energized, she reached for the phone. She could go to her aunt and uncle in Fairmont. They lived in the mountains — she'd be safe there. Luke could go with her. Her aunt and uncle wouldn't mind.

She punched in Luke's number. She had no doubt he would be awake. He answered on the first ring.

"Luke, we have to get out of here, out of town," Mandy said in a rush. "This time I didn't just black out, I had the most horrific nightmare. My brain is telling me it's had enough. I have some cool relatives in Fairmont. We can go there until they find out what's causing the power surges."

Silence.

"Luke?"

"Mandy, we can't leave. Something terrible is going to happen. We might be the only ones who can stop it."

"Oh, Luke." Mandy sighed. "One night away from this, one good night's sleep and you'll know how crazy this sounds."

"I know all about your 'nightmare,' Mandy. I know because *I was there*. In the ship. With the dyzychs." In a relentless voice, Luke described her nightmare. At length. In detail.

Mandy felt as if her insides were slowly turning to stone. A terrible lethargy crept over her. Her ear felt frozen to the phone.

She fought back. Her mind scrambled for the right words. Words to end this. "We're sharing hallucinations, Luke," she insisted, her argument forming as she spoke. "Quentin is doing it. He's found a way to focus on us, terrorize us simultaneously."

"Okay, fine," Luke spat. "If you can explain

to me how he drilled our skulls simultaneously in our dreams."

Mandy's temple began to throb. Her hand flew up. She felt a small scab. And a little ridge, as if the plug of bone hadn't been set quite flush with her skull.

Inside her head, a voice began to laugh.

The phone dropped from her hand.

Chapter Twenty-seven

Luke hung up. His insides were in turmoil. He'd give Mandy a while to get used to the idea, then call her back.

A plan was forming in his mind, but he needed her help.

His attention was caught by a sound on the stairs. Footsteps. Jeff. Making no particular effort to be quiet. But Mom and Dad would be relieved that at least he was home.

Luke waited until he heard his brother's bedroom door open. Then he followed him. "Hi, Jeff. Can I come in?"

Jeff was seated on his bed, taking off his heavy, black Doc Marten boots. He shrugged.

Luke pushed himself off the door frame. He grabbed Jeff's desk chair and straddled it backwards. Although it had been six months, Luke still got a jolt when he looked at his little brother's bald head.

Jeff had been kind of a chubby kid with rosy cheeks. A baby face. He'd grown out of the flab and the face, but maybe he figured this new look would make sure that angelic boy was banished forever.

"Did I wake you from your beauty sleep?" Jeff sneered. The lightning-bolt tattoo zagged like the real thing. One boot hit the floor.

"I was awake," Luke said, keeping his voice neutral. It was so easy for Jeff to get him going. "What have you been up to tonight?"

Jeff jerked his head up suspiciously. "What's it to you?"

"Just curious. You been out with Quentin?"

Briefly, Jeff looked blank. As though he couldn't remember who he'd been with, and only this minute realized it.

Luke's pulse began to quicken. "Did he try any of that mind stuff on you? Hypnosis or whatever it is?"

Jeff frowned belligerently. "It's none of your business what I do."

Luke forced a laugh. "No. I guess Quentin figures it's none of *your* business either. You don't even remember where you've been tonight, do you?"

"Sure I do." Jeff's eyes refused to meet his. "But I sure don't have to tell you." His second boot came off suddenly. Fine grit poured out onto the floor. Grit from the quarry.

"No. I guess Quentin doesn't tell you much. I bet he hasn't even told you about the Others."

"I want to get some sleep."

"Do you even know who the Others are? How about the dyzychs?"

Jeff yawned wider and lay back.

Luke changed his tactics. "Your gang's been getting smaller lately, have you noticed? Quentin leads some kids off and they never come back. Strange, isn't it? Don't you want to know what's going to happen when it's your turn? Or do you just follow, like a sheep?"

Jeff came up off the bed. "You don't know anything. The Q is onto something big. Some kind of mission. He's promised to get me out of this stupid town for good. And I know he can do it. You'll be laughing out of the other side of your face pretty soon, bro."

Luke felt excitement building in his gut. He was getting somewhere now. If he could just keep Jeff talking. But if he goaded him any further, Jeff might throw him out.

"I'm not laughing," Luke started to say. But the words stuck in his throat.

Suddenly he felt like his head was splitting in two. Half his brain shut down.

The other half went crazy.

Chapter Twenty-eight

The laughter in Mandy's head welled up from a dark place. Like an unknown cave in the center of her brain.

At first chillingly faint, the laughter grew louder. It began to shoot up from inside her, exerting tremendous pressure.

The laughter wasn't hers. But it was familiar in a sinister way.

The laughter was Quentin's.

It was not a memory. Somehow it was *there*, inside her.

The sound throbbed with diabolical joy.

Mandy's brain shrank from a horror she couldn't fully comprehend. It filled her skull until she felt her head would burst.

"I am here, Mandy sweets."

The voice, though oily quiet, ripped through her like a claw hammer.

"Oh, that was good. It's almost like terror

has a mental taste. I had no idea. My previous experience of the phenomenon pales in comparison."

Mandy floundered. Nothing existed but the overwhelming horror of this moment, this instant. There was no escape.

"None, Mandy. That's right, I know everything you're thinking." Inside her head, Quentin's voice was almost playful. *"You are mine in a way that surpasses your wildest dreams. Or should I say nightmares? Ain't technology great?"*

Mandy felt like a big, beached fish. Gasping and totally helpless. Even her fragmented thoughts were lost to her.

"We're going to make use of our new intimacy, Mandy. We are going to —"

There was a staticky jolt. Quentin's presence flickered. Mandy felt his burst of anger. But it didn't sear her skull.

More static.

"What do you mean it was too soon?" he cried furiously, speaking to someone else. *"Fix it. I'm losing her."*

Mandy's mind rushed together. Her thoughts raced in a panic to fill the dark place — as if they might somehow block Quentin's invasion. But Mandy knew they wouldn't.

She shook her head, trying to help dislodge the dyzych device. It had no effect.

She felt static mostly, little jolts like deep itches she couldn't scratch. And spurts of Quentin's anger, which sparked peaks of panicky terror every time.

And another presence. The dyzych. It was a deep, cold alien presence that inspired a paralyzing terror.

It was detached, not like Quentin's visceral hatred.

All these things sputtered in her, grabbing and letting go. Her head was full of meaningless white noise. Her own thoughts surfaced desperately in the brief interludes of quiet.

Hours passed. Or maybe seconds. Mandy didn't know.

She felt wrung out.

But she no longer had any doubts about the alien invasion.

A sudden surge of current flipped her backwards onto her bed. Her brain felt hot. Like she was burning up from inside.

And then — nothing. It was all gone: the static, the voices, the presences.

Mandy jumped up, surprised to find she already knew what she was going to do. Underneath Quentin and the static, her brain had never stopped working. This made her feel almost hopeful.

She was going to go to the hospital. She was

going to get them to X-ray her head and remove the implant.

Mandy grabbed up the phone. As she punched Luke's number, she noticed it was daylight. Almost nine o'clock. So many hours gone. So many hours dead.

Luke didn't answer. Mandy clenched her fist against her knee. She didn't know how much time she had. Five seconds, five minutes, an hour.

"Luke, where are you?" she muttered in anguish. And realized she was talking to his answering machine. She was afraid to leave a message.

Maybe that was silly. The implant could switch on any second. Then Quentin would have her. Luke wouldn't know where she had gone.

She'd stop by his house. Maybe he'd be back by then. If not, she could leave him a note. She could only hope that Luke wasn't in any danger yet.

Maybe the dyzych would leave Luke alone until they needed him.

Mandy stuck paper and pencil in her pocket and then set off at a jog, unaware of her surroundings and the occasional curious glance her disheveled, mismatched appearance attracted.

The fear pounded along beside her. She monitored her brain, too conscious of her utter helplessness. The voice — the static — could come back at any time.

She turned onto Luke's street, feeling the delay pressing on her. Knocking on the front door, she called up to his open window, "Luke!"

Mandy was digging the paper out of her pocket when she heard something inside.

Footsteps padded across the floor. The door opened.

"Oh!" Mandy gasped. She'd forgotten about the younger brother.

His blank eyes fastened on her.

The lightning bolt on his face zagged when he smiled.

Chapter Twenty-nine

Upstairs, Luke lay on his back in bed. His arms were rigid at his sides.

Mandy's anguished voice on the telephone still echoed in his ears. "Luke, where are you?"

He had tried to get to the phone. He had strained to pick it up. But all his efforts produced was a jumpy twitch in his fingers.

Now he heard Mandy's voice drift up to him, calling his name. He heard his brother go downstairs, heard the door open.

Luke put all his strength into calling out a warning. But no sound emerged from his paralyzed throat.

"Do you know where he went?"

He couldn't make out Jeff's answer. He heard Mandy enter the house. Inwardly, he thrashed and fought. Outwardly, he could have been a corpse. Except for the sweat that broke out on his brow.

"Well, can I leave him a note?"

"Sure."

A minute later the front door closed. Footsteps came unhurriedly up. His bedroom door opened.

Without looking at Luke, Jeff dropped the folded note on his chest. He turned and went out, shutting the door behind him.

Luke couldn't see the note. But a bright point of relief stood out in his sea of despair. Mandy was free.

He couldn't think beyond that. He couldn't think about why or how long she would stay free. His mind was filled with a cold busyness, like a million ants trampling though his gray matter.

The dyzychs had pushed Luke aside in his own head. As if his presence was an insignificant nuisance. His terror beneath notice.

Somehow he knew the dyzychs were exploring. He was being dissected from the inside out. His heart sped, then slowed. A muscle contracted in one leg, then the other. They were learning him. Getting the feel of a human body.

Getting ready to take over.

Luke lost track of time. Waves of cold washed over him again and again. His body twitched and spasmed.

Then the activity stopped. Luke felt heavy — all the strength had been sucked from his limbs.

Something was happening. Luke convulsed. His arm shot up, then fell back again.

He could feel the cold alien satisfaction. It had him under control.

Then it began to spread, seizing Luke's brain for itself. Slowly, steadily, Luke felt himself being squeezed. He was disappearing into the alien maw. It was steadily pressing him into a tiny corner of his own consciousness.

Luke pushed and struggled, fighting for space. His own brain was crushing him.

Suddenly he found himself sitting. The room whirled, tilted, righted itself. His eyes rolled back in his head, straining to see. His sight was diminished to a narrow band.

But it wasn't. He could see fine. With a leap of terror that made him slip his tenuous hold, Luke realized his thoughts were mixing in with the alien's.

He, Luke, was seeing normally. The alien was not. As the dyzych struggled with Luke's human eyes, Luke realized that dyzych eyes would take in almost the whole room. It would see dust on the ceiling as clearly as the pattern of his bedspread.

Luke fought to regain his tiny perch. To lift himself out of the whirlpool of alien thought. He flailed in panic. And was startled to find himself standing.

His fingers were holding Mandy's note. There was a new voice in his head.

"You have no conception of how much I'm enjoying myself, Luke." Quentin. The purr of evil made the dyzych presence seem benign. *"You're going to do something for me now. You are going to hate it. Really hate it. You're going to go kicking, screaming, and sobbing, but you will go.*

"You're going to bring Mandy to me."

Luke's nerveless fingers were unfolding the note. He strained to keep his eyes from reading it. He could feel Quentin's amusement at his feeble efforts.

The note said: "Luke, I'm going to see my mother at work. Come as soon as you can." This last sentence was crossed out. "Come NOW," Mandy had written instead, underlining it so hard the pencil had torn the paper.

"And that's exactly what you are going to do, Luke old pal." Luke could feel Quentin's breath of satisfaction blow through him like wind off a sewer. *"For now, it's back to dyzych command central. Be seeing you. Soon."*

Quentin, with a little savage dig of satisfaction, informed the dyzych where Mandy was.

"Her mother works at the hospital. If you don't succeed in getting her out of there, they'll find the implant," Quentin explained with mali-

cious relish. *"So right now our interests in collecting Mandy are completely equal, and yours are rather more urgent than my own."*

Immediately Luke felt the alien seize him. He turned toward the bedroom door, lumbering like a zombie.

The stairs almost ended the mission. Stepping down onto the first one, Luke felt his leg bend backwards. The alien was going to turn his knee joint inside out!

A burst of pain shot up his leg. Overcompensating, the alien missed the step entirely with Luke's other foot. Luke felt himself topple.

Suddenly strength flooded back into his limbs. Luke immediately took control. The alien presence had fled.

Instinctively, Luke grabbed the banister, stopping his fall.

His brain worked feverishly. He had to get to his phone and call Mandy at the hospital. He had to warn her. He turned to bolt back to his room.

Instantly, like the flick of a switch, the dyzych returned.

Luke lashed out. But the alien already had him turned around. Taking the steps down, one at a time.

Luke heard Jeff come quietly out of his room. He tried to shout, but the noise only echoed in his head. His hand reached out and opened the front door.

As Luke went out, he glimpsed Jeff standing at the top of the stairs. Watching.

Still awkward, jerked along by an inexperienced puppeteer, Luke went down the front walk.

At the street, he turned toward the hospital.

Chapter Thirty

Mandy pushed open the door to the emergency room. There weren't many people waiting. Mandy went up to the desk feeling, for the first time, like she might make it.

A little boy with too much energy was dashing around, applying a big horseshoe magnet to everything he saw. While she waited for someone to come, Mandy watched him indulgently.

Sometimes it seemed like a million years since she'd been a little kid like that. Other times it seemed like the blink of an eye. She still had her own magnet collection on the beaten strip of iron over her bed.

If she had to wait, she figured she might as well show the little boy some of her magnet tricks.

Suddenly there was a blare of static in her head. A cold presence flooded her. Dyzych. It grabbed her roughly. Mandy felt herself flung into a corner of her own skull.

Vaguely, she was aware of the little boy zooming by. He aimed his magnet at her and made shooting noises.

Another burst of inner static jarred her. The dyzych vanished, cut off. But now it knew where she was.

"Mandy?"

Mandy jumped in panic. A nurse was regarding her quizzically. "Are you looking for your mother?"

Mandy gulped in some air, trying to control her trembling. "Ah, no." Mandy cleared her throat. She told herself it wouldn't hurt to look a little wigged out.

"Actually, I haven't mentioned anything about this to her," she said. "I didn't want to worry her. But I fell a couple days ago and since then I've been feeling nauseous and getting terrible headaches. Dizzy, too. It seems worse today and I thought I should get a head X ray."

The nurse looked instantly concerned. As she should. Mandy had just described the symptoms of a concussion.

"Right this way," the nurse said. "Tell me, did you feel dizzy before you fell? Or not until afterwards?"

Mandy hesitated. "I'm not sure," she said. "Maybe. I can't remember very well."

As she'd hoped, the nurse walked a little more briskly, signaling for a doctor as she settled Mandy into an examining cubicle.

The doctor, a woman about her mother's age with short, graying hair and friendly eyes, asked a bunch of medical questions. If Mandy wasn't sure how to answer, she said she couldn't remember.

The doctor shined a light in Mandy's eyes and tested her reflexes. "I don't see any signs of concussion," she said. "But we'll take an X ray to be safe."

When the doctor left, Mandy felt a savage triumph. She had beaten them. Quentin couldn't get her now. She was in the hands of the medical establishment.

If she started acting bizarre and trying to escape, they'd hold her all the more firmly. Soon they would find that thing in her brain. And soon after that, the world would know.

There would be FBI or whoever swarming all over the town. The aliens would lose.

The doctor returned, with Mandy's anxious mother in tow. Usually Mandy hated being fussed over, but this time she basked in it.

After the X ray was taken, Mandy sat in the radiology lab waiting room. Her mother had gone back to work.

What if they didn't find the implant? She began to worry, but she didn't have long to wait.

The doctor who had first examined her entered the waiting room, smiling uncertainly. "You don't seem to be concussed," she said. "But we want to have the radiologist examine your films. We may need to take some more."

"Is there a problem?" Mandy asked, almost slumping with relief. They had found the implant. Now they would remove it. She did her best to look worried, since that's what the doctor would expect.

"I'm sure there isn't," the doctor said in that infuriating way they had. "Please, come this way."

Mandy was led to an examining room. A handsome young doctor, blond with an athletic physique, entered. For some reason, Mandy's nerves began to prickle with anxiety. What was going on?

The doctor smiled. There was something familiar about his eyes. "I've already explained to the others it was nothing, just a glitch in the film," he said.

Then he grinned at her, his eyes glittering strangely.

"A glitch?" Mandy tried to keep the nervousness out of her voice. "Are you sure? Maybe you should take another X ray?" If she had to, she could get her mom to insist.

The doctor let his eyes rove over her in a very nonmedical way. Mandy jumped off the examining table, alarm bells suddenly jangling in her head.

"That's, um, good news." Even to her own ears, her voice sounded shrill. "I'll go tell my mother."

The doctor stepped closer. "These X rays are actually very interesting." He stuck the tip of his purplish tongue between his teeth as he examined the film. "Amazing work they do, isn't it?" A raspy note of irritation crept into his modulated voice. "Not perfect, obviously. But I'm assured a little fine tuning is all that's required."

"They?" echoed Mandy. Chills raced up and down her spine.

He was standing between her and the closed door. She calculated her chances of getting past him. Not good. She'd have to create a distraction.

"Oh, I think we both know what I'm talking about," the handsome doctor said with oily satisfaction. The professional smoothness of his voice cracked.

Mandy froze in horror. It couldn't be.

"Their technology is vastly superior. As are their physical attributes," he added, as his purple tongue protruded farther and farther. "Such wonders we have in store for you."

He slipped his hand inside the white doctor's coat. He brought out a long silvery instrument.

He grinned at Mandy and scratched his eyebrow with the pointed tip of his tongue.

Mandy bit back a scream. Her pulse hammered. It was now or never.

She lashed out with her foot, connecting hard with his knee.

"Ooof!" yelled the doctor, his eyes bugging furiously.

His blond hair began to dissolve.

Mandy dashed for the door. She was reaching for the doorknob when her head seemed to split open.

The alien implant had activated again.

Her eyes skewed in different directions. Her body froze. Half her mind was blinking in disoriented amazement. The other half — the normal half — was petrified with shock. Her eyesight reeled around the room in a whirling blur.

Mandy focused all her energy into her will. If she didn't regain control now, while the implant device was off balance, she wouldn't get a second chance.

Straining, she tugged her eyesight free of the alien's hold. She concentrated on her hand and ordered it to move. The hand lifted. Mandy looked at the doorknob. "Open it," she commanded herself.

She could hear the "doctor" groaning and muttering curses behind her. Her hand inched forward. It felt like she was moving a two-hundred-pound weight.

Behind her there was an angry growl. Fear jolted through her.

Inside her head, the alien was getting its bearings. She felt as if the creature was digging grasping claws into her brain.

Mandy reached for the doorknob with all her might. Her hand jerked forward and grasped the doorknob. Turning it took all of her strength. Almost there. Another inch.

Suddenly the doorknob twisted in her hand. The door flew open, smashing her backwards.

The alien in her mind surged forward, seizing her brain. Mandy lost her balance and fell to the floor.

"What's going on in here?" asked the nurse who had opened the door. "Is she all right? I heard what sounded like yelling."

"She's having some kind of fit," said the doctor, crouching beside her. His glittery eyes looked into Mandy's, full of cold triumph. The blond hair was back in place, his face re-arranged in smooth professional planes.

"We'll have to admit her. And, nurse, we'll need to use restraints. Help me get her back on the table."

The alien presence squatted in the center of Mandy's mind. She was boxed into a tiny corner, totally aware, totally helpless.

She was lifted back onto the table. Cold terror washed through her as the restraint bands were bound tightly over her. Her heart thumped against her constricted chest.

Now, even if she got control of her mind, she was still helpless.

There was one shred of hope. Her note to Luke. He'd save her.

She prayed he was on his way.

Chapter Thirty-one

Luke lurched along the sidewalk.

He could feel the alien's exasperation as it tried to steer his awkward bulk.

Luke's foot caught in a crack. His body stumbled, beginning the long fall down. The alien jerked upward, unable to find Luke's balance.

Seizing his chance, Luke battered at his coffinlike prison with all his strength. He pushed and kicked and punched.

His body hit the sidewalk. Pain jolted up his arm and burned in his right leg.

With a rush of fury, the alien batted Luke aside. A dark blot, it pinned Luke into a space so tiny he couldn't move. Panic raked him as the alien pressed. He was going to be crushed out of existence.

Terrified, Luke went still. The alien's anger washed over him.

But once Luke stopped thrashing, the dyzych

turned its attention to Luke's body. It couldn't seem to get the hang of knee joints.

The pain was excruciating, even for Luke, although his body now felt removed from him completely.

Eventually, his body was back on its feet.

Luke decided to stop fighting. It was doing him no good and was draining his mental energy.

It might be wiser to concentrate on learning about the alien.

As his body staggered along toward the hospital, Luke studied its cold presence.

With a jolt, he realized the alien's fury toward him was not personal. The dyzych only lashed out in frustration, much like a person might kick at the tire of a car that broke down.

The alien could crush him in a temper fit and think no more of it than Luke would about crumpling a soda can.

This understanding terrified him in a way that a personal attack could not.

Curled in his sliver of brain space, Luke wondered if Quentin had ever experienced the icy objectivity of the dyzych consciousness.

Quentin thought of other people as objects, but Luke knew, deep in his soul, that the dyzychs thought of all humanity — including their ally Quentin — as things, not real living beings.

Perhaps that was how they found their human allies. Depraved creatures like Quentin, who considered humans only as their usefulness applied to him.

To the dyzychs, Quentin's sadistic pleasure in human pain would be incomprehensible. They would indulge it, but only as far as it didn't inconvenience them.

And this particular dyzych was beginning to feel inconvenienced.

Turning Luke's body up the ramp to the hospital entrance, the alien miscalculated. Luke's knee wrenched. A spurt of white hot dyzych anger erupted.

And another revelation exploded in Luke's mind. The dyzych found the human body not just clumsy, but disgusting!

Human bones and pulsing, messy organs revolted them.

Quentin's self-loathing and loathing for others must have seemed attractive, possibly even sympathetic. But still, they knew he was human and could be enticed with disgusting human rewards.

Like clear skin and lustrous hair. A slight variation in the crude human form. His will imposed over others of his loathsome kind.

Luke staggered through the hospital's automatic doors. He stopped, swaying, while the dyzych got its bearings. The alien's annoyance was a steady simmer now.

It walked Luke to the information desk. "I. Want. To. See. Mandy. Durgin." The alien didn't have full control over Luke's vocal cords. His voice was jerky and raspy.

The woman behind the desk looked at him with some alarm. Luke hoped the dyzych wouldn't be able to read her face. This woman would never direct them to Mandy. Right now she was probably calculating how quick she could get to security.

"I'll just check on that," the woman said in the sort of soothing voice medical people used on lunatics. "If you'll take a seat over there, please."

Dyzych irritation cranked up another notch. He jerked Luke around and parked his body in a molded plastic chair.

A small boy was looking at him over the crook of his mother's restraining arm. Luke would have liked to smile, but the dyzych kept his face stony.

Luke tried to figure out how he could use what he had learned so far. Nothing came to him. Security would be arriving soon. But that wouldn't give him more than a few minutes respite.

He knew the dyzych was determined to get

Mandy out, and it wouldn't care what happened to Luke's body in the process.

Suddenly Luke jerked as a hammer blow struck the inside of his skull. The dyzych clenched Luke's teeth against a groan. Luke felt its fury might burn him up, almost accidentally.

"Sorry," came a new, impatient voice, sounding not at all sorry. Quentin. *"I didn't have time for finesse. We've got to hurry."*

Even as Luke groped wildly for an idea that might help him, he felt his hopes draining away. He sensed that Quentin knew all about the dyzych's disgust and disinterest — and it didn't bother him a bit.

Quentin had something the dyzych needed. And that was all that mattered to any of them. If only Quentin would let slip what it was, maybe then Luke would have a weapon to use against him.

"I've got Mandy immobilized in radiology. I've even been able to remove the restraints," Quentin added in a tone that made Luke go cold. *"All we need now is the packhorse. Luke. Let me have the reins."*

Luke felt a tug. *"It'll be quicker if I guide him,"* Quentin insisted. *"There's no time to waste. Mandy's mother will be here in minutes and that will complicate things. We might have to eliminate her."*

The little boy suddenly broke free of his mother. He ran straight at Luke, his big horseshoe magnet stretched out in front of him.

"*Stupid kid,*" Quentin said impatiently. "*Snarl at him and he'll run back to mama.*"

The dyzych seemed puzzled. In the second he hesitated, the charging boy had reached Luke. He banged into his knee and held up the magnet.

"*Hurr —*"

But Quentin's command was suddenly cut off. The dyzych presence winked out.

Luke gasped. A deep, heaving breath of shock. His consciousness expanded to flood his body's every cell.

He was free! But how?

The little kid with the magnet dashed away.

Luke started to his feet. He had to get to Mandy, warn the doctors about Quentin.

Suddenly he lost control again. Luke staggered and fell back in the chair, his head dizzy with warring voices.

The alien's anger stung like a whiplash.

"*I didn't do anything,*" Quentin whined. "*Mandy's implant failed, too. That's how we got in this mess. Your devices don't work —*"

The little boy zoomed by again, waving his magnet.

A burst of static disrupted the voices. And again Luke seized his body. His eyes followed the child wonderingly. As the boy ran farther away, white static blared in Luke's head.

"Hey, kid," Luke called out desperately. "Can I see your magnet?"

The dyzych's anger seared him as Quentin and the alien wrestled for control.

The boy approached warily. He stuck his thumb in his mouth and stopped.

Luke reached out with a tremendous effort. He wrenched his lips into a smile. "Let me see," he begged, his voice strangled.

The child handed Luke the magnet. The alien static inside his mind ceased. Luke pressed the magnet to his head. It worked!

"Hey, what's going on here?"

Luke looked up.

The boy's mother was standing before him, scowling, holding her kid's hand protectively. "What are you doing with my son's toy?"

Luke's mind felt stretched beyond endurance. There was no way he was giving the magnet back.

The magnet. It disrupted the implant. It disrupted Quentin's psychic projections, too. He couldn't let it go.

"I — I have these horrible headaches," Luke said, thinking so fast his brain hurt. "So bad I can hardly walk. But the magnet took the pain away."

The woman stared at him in disbelief. But it

didn't matter if she thought he was crazy. Just so long as she knew he was harmless.

"Please. The gift shop might have some refrigerator magnets. Nice ones," Luke said earnestly. "Walk me there and I'll buy some. I'll give your son his magnet back plus some new ones."

"There's no need for that," the woman said, her stance relaxing slightly. Clearly she felt sorry for him. "We'll go to the gift shop with you."

Luke bought every magnet the shop had. He bought a bunch of bandanas, too. He let the little boy pick out a fish and a bunny magnet and gave him back his horseshoe.

Once the boy and his mother were gone, Luke ripped all the cute little animal decorations off the magnets, wrapped them in two bandanas, and tied one around his head. The other he stuffed in his pocket, already hurrying toward radiology.

A nurse looked up as he entered. Her eyes widened slightly.

Luke supposed he must look deranged with his torn jeans and bloody knee from the fall on the way here, as well as the lumpy bandana tied around his head. He asked for Mandy.

"She's not receiving visitors at the moment," the nurse said stiffly. But Luke saw her eyes cut to a closed examining room door down the hall. "Her mother is coming down, if you want to wait for her."

Luke dashed down the hall.

"Hey! Stop!"

By the time the nurse got out from behind her desk, he'd be inside with Mandy. He only needed enough time to press the magnets to her head.

Doubt flashed in his mind. What if the magnet thing had been a fluke? Maybe the implant had just stopped working. It could start up again any time.

Luke flung open the examining room door. There was a straight-backed chair beside the door. He quickly grabbed it and shoved it under the doorknob.

Only then did he notice there were two people in the room. The blond doctor gave him a shock.

But Luke whipped the other bundle of magnets out of his pocket. He pushed past the doctor without looking at him. Mandy's face was slack. He shivered and pressed the bandana to her head.

Alarm jumped in her eyes. "Quentin!" she yelled urgently. "He's Quentin! Look out!"

Luke spun. The blond doctor's face rippled. Luke blinked and saw Quentin's snarl. And then the heavy metal tool he was holding crashed down on Luke's skull.

Pain blossomed. Black spots distorted his vision. But Luke sidestepped. He couldn't fall now. To go down would mean death.

He heard Mandy's feet hit the floor as she jumped off the table.

"Get the window open," he told her. "We'll go out that way."

There was a tall window, covered with mini-blinds. As Quentin rushed him, Luke heard Mandy yank the blinds and unlatch the window.

Someone pounded on the door and called out. The chair under the doorknob slid an inch across the floor.

Quentin slashed the air where Luke's head had been an instant before. Quentin's momentum carried him forward, past Luke.

Luke slipped behind him and grabbed his arm, yanking the elbow backwards.

Quentin's cry of pain and rage was like that of a rabid animal. Luke grabbed another bandana from his pocket. Now he knew why he had bought extra bandanas.

Moving quickly, Luke wrapped the bandana around Quentin's wrists and tied it securely. Not as good as handcuffs, maybe, but it worked.

Voices were yelling outside the door. The chair scraped roughly and gave another few inches.

Luke's heart pounded wildly. They had to run. If Quentin could impersonate a doctor and hypnotize everyone into seeing him that way, the hospital was too dangerous.

He sprang for the window. Mandy was half out, waiting.

"Mandy." Quentin's voice was a command.

Mandy's head jerked around in obedience.

"Stop him."

Her body went rigid.

Luke's heart twisted. The bandana with the magnets. It had come loose, fallen somewhere.

The chair screamed another inch across the floor. "Open this door," an angry man's voice demanded.

"Mandy," her mother called from outside the door.

Luke's eyes went to the examining table. He couldn't see where the magnets had fallen. There was no time, they'd have to do without. He could carry her out.

In a stride, Luke was at the window. Mandy's head snapped toward him. Her face was dead.

Except for her eyes. Her eyes were wide with fear.

"Come on, Mandy." Luke grabbed her hand. "It'll be okay."

She wrenched it from his grasp. Her arms reached for him. Relieved, Luke moved into their embrace.

Mandy's hands closed around his neck.

Anguish welled up in her eyes.

She squeezed.

Luke choked.

The chair squealed across the floor. It fell with a crash.

Mrs. Durgin entered the room and screamed. "What are you doing to my daughter?"

Tears rolled down Mandy's cheeks.

She squeezed harder.

Chapter Thirty-two

Mandy watched Luke's eyes bulge out.

Her knuckles whitened as she pressed her fingers into his throat.

She screamed inside her mind, but there was no one to hear. No one except Quentin. His fury burned. He was enjoying himself.

Luke started to crumple. A blur of people crowded into the room.

The urge to flee leaped in her. But this time it was Quentin's order. "*Out,*" he commanded. "*Run.*"

She let go of Luke and braced herself to jump from the window. Out of the corner of her eye, she saw Luke scoop something red from the floor. A distraction. Quentin's thought. "*Go.*"

Luke's hand came up and reached for her even though she had tried to strangle him.

Mandy jumped. Luke leaped after her. A blur of noise in her head.

Then freedom.

Quentin's hold snapped like a frayed rubber band.

Luke held the red cloth to her head like a compress. "Magnets," he said, looking feverishly over his shoulder. "They disrupt the implant somehow. Tie this on. Hurry."

Her mind flashed to the strip of dancing animals over her bed. Her childhood magnet collection. The magnets had been small and not close enough to her head. But slowly it had worked. And lasted a long time.

Then the boy in the waiting room. Comprehension dawned. She should have known.

People were yelling behind them. "Mandy!" her mother screamed.

Mandy quickly tied the bandana around her neck. "This will do it," she said. "Trust me."

"Okay, then. Run. He's coming."

Mandy threw a glance backwards. His arms freed, Quentin was stumbling out the window after them. His hair wavered from blond to dark.

"Sorry, Mom," Mandy called. "He wants to hurt me!"

"I know, Mandy." Her mother's haunted eyes fixed on Luke. "I'm coming, baby!" She started climbing awkwardly over the windowsill.

"No," yelled Mandy. "Not Luke! The fake doctor. Stop him!"

There was a bellow of anger from Quentin. Mandy glimpsed her mother being thrown to the ground as Quentin pushed her out of his way.

Mandy and Luke fled across the hospital grounds. The area around the buildings was wide open. Nothing but grass. No place to hide. Mandy felt her breath rasp in her lungs.

A movement off to the side caught her eyes.

Skinheads! They were coming around the building, trying to cut them off.

Mandy risked a glance backwards.

Quentin was hot on their heels. He hadn't gained any ground, but he hadn't lost ground either. And they hadn't had much of a head start.

"He'll never catch us," Luke gasped. "He has no endurance."

Mandy couldn't help picturing the alien machinery efficiently vacuuming bones and replacing them with something better.

She was sure Quentin was in whatever shape he wanted to be.

"The — *chuff* — skinheads' boots — *pant* — are too heavy," said Luke. "They won't catch us."

Mandy saved her breath for running. They raced across the grass toward the nearest cluster of houses. The expanse of empty lawn seemed to go on forever.

Mandy's legs felt rubbery. Her breath was so loud in her ears she knew she'd never hear Quentin come up behind her until he grabbed her. The thought was terrifying. She glanced back.

He was gaining!

Mandy didn't think she could run faster, but fear pumped her heart like rocket fuel.

She stumbled. She caught herself and kept running, but she had lost precious distance. She could practically feel Quentin's icy breath cold on her neck.

But the houses were getting nearer. She summoned energy out of nothing and found a spurt of speed.

"I know — *pant, pant* — this — *pant* — neighborhood," Luke managed, not realizing how far back she had fallen. She could barely hear him. "We'll — *pant* — lose them."

They reached a four-foot chain-link fence and Luke sailed over it like it wasn't there. It looked impossibly high. Mandy heard the pound of boots behind her. She cleared the fence.

The impact when she hit the ground was brain jarring.

"Mandy," Luke croaked. "Hurry!"

Energy sparked at her heels. Behind them she heard grunts and curses as the skinheads tried to fit the reinforced toes of their boots into the fence links.

Luke headed for another fence, and Mandy flew right over it with him.

They zigzagged through the neighborhood, backyard to backyard, steering clear of streets.

They lost the last of the skinheads after the third fence, but Luke didn't slow down. Quentin was still back there somewhere.

Mandy's lungs ached. Her ankle throbbed where she'd banged it on a high wooden fence with no toeholds. They had taken so many twists and turns, her sense of direction was shot.

Finally, just when she thought she was going to collapse, Luke stopped. He leaned up against a big oak in somebody's backyard, chest heaving.

"I don't hear anyone, do you?" he asked between big gulping breaths.

The blood was pounding so hard in her ears, Mandy didn't know what she heard. She gestured to Luke and they crouched down and squeezed themselves under a thick hedge.

No one came by.

But they both knew that Quentin hadn't stopped looking.

"You know where we have to go next, don't you?" Luke asked.

Mandy nodded. "Quentin's house. The last place he'll think to look for us."

Chapter Thirty-three

"Right," Luke said. "Quentin's house. There might be some clue where we can find the ship."

His gut clenched. He wished he had some idea what they were going to do if — no, *when* — they found the ship.

"He's such an arrogant show-off, he probably keeps a map on his bedroom wall," Mandy observed.

There was a smudge of dirt on her nose. Luke took out one of his extra bandanas to wipe it away.

Mandy looked at him, her eyes searching his face. "Luke, if we find the ship, we're not going to try to be heroes are we? We'll go and get help, right?"

"Sure." An excellent idea. Luke only hoped they would get the chance to put it to work.

They crawled out from under the hedge and picked their way carefully through a flower bed. They had trampled a lot of flowers in the course of their flight. If they got through this, a lot of angry gardeners would be calling his mother and yelling their heads off.

Luke smiled to himself. It would be nice to be worried about something as simple as that.

He led the way, keeping to backyards and away from the streets. They halted frequently to watch and listen. Once, a pair of skinheads came hustling by on the street. Luckily, their clomping was so loud that Luke and Mandy could tell they were coming and had time to hide.

As they waited for their skinhead hunters to pass, Mandy fingered the little magnets in the bandana bundle around her neck.

"The solution was so simple," she marveled. "It must work the way a magnet messes up a compass heading."

"Or the way it erases a computer disk," Luke said, craning his neck to see where their pursuers had gone. "Okay, they're gone."

They spied two more skinhead groups and had plenty of time to evade them. "These kids have no concept of quiet," said Mandy, almost cheerily.

Mandy and Luke slowed as they approached Quentin's backyard. Luke's skin began to crawl. What if Quentin was here, waiting for his soldiers to report in?

There were tall bushes along the property line, screening them from neighbors. But Luke felt horribly exposed as they pushed into the backyard and crossed the lawn.

Luke knocked on the back door. "To make sure nobody's home," he explained. They pressed themselves against the side of the house, wishing for thicker landscaping.

"Get ready to run if someone opens the door," Luke whispered.

They waited for what seemed an eternity. No one came.

They crept back to the door. No surprise it was locked.

"I noticed an open window," Mandy volunteered. She pointed at a small window, about shoulder height. "Just my size," she muttered.

Luke bent the screen a little in order to pop it out. The noise he made was excruciating. Again they waited, pressed against the house, hearts pounding.

Luke felt time slipping away. But when he glanced at his watch, he found that less than five minutes had passed since they had stepped onto Quentin's property.

"I think it's okay," Mandy whispered.

Luke gave her a boost up. It was a tight fit. Mandy grunted softly as she hauled herself through. When her legs disappeared inside, Luke had a hollow moment of panic.

But then the back door opened and Mandy, white-faced and wide-eyed, was gesturing him inside.

The house had the silence of emptiness. Evil emptiness.

Luke straightened the screen and replaced it in the window.

He was already shaking. Mandy was, too. Luke wiped his sweaty palms on his shorts. They were both scared half out of their minds.

"It feels so creepy," Mandy whispered.

"I know," Luke said, equally hushed. "I suppose we should separate." His eyes darted nervously around the kitchen and out into the hall. "It'll go faster."

"No." Mandy shook her head vehemently. "I'm not creeping around on my own. If there's anything here, it'll be in Quentin's room."

Luke didn't argue. He was actually relieved to have her beside him as they went down the hall and started upstairs, careful to make no sound.

Mandy jumped when a pipe gurgled somewhere. And Luke's heart was racing. He expected Quentin to jump out at them any moment, whipping his mutant tongue.

At the top of the stairs, they stopped and looked around. There was a hallway with four doors off it, three of them open. The fourth was closed. A sign on it read, in big block letters:

Luke wiped his palms again. Sweat trickled down his neck. He stepped forward and opened the door.

Quentin's room was surprisingly neat.

Mandy followed him in. They gaped in silence at the walls. A huge collage, mostly pictures cut from magazines. It turned Mandy's blood to ice.

The pictures had all been cut up and put back together in grotesque ways. There was a pig with a man's head. A horse with no legs. A man with six arms and a duck's webbed feet. A woman with two heads and no arms.

It was sick, totally sick.

Luke made a hoarse sound and grabbed Mandy's arm.

There in a corner, almost lost in a mess of other photos, was a snapshot of Mandy. She was standing in a group of *X-Files* aliens. Her smiling head had been cut off and stuck onto the body of an alien.

Luke was there, too. In a picture taken from the yearbook. His face was grinning, but his arms and legs had been cut off. Behind him was another alien, its mouth yawning open, poised to swallow Luke's head.

There was a second picture of Luke. Just his head, this time. Quentin had pasted it to a cartoon body of a man with his heart cut out.

Luke's stomach twisted. "He's even more of a psycho than I thought," he said.

Mandy shuddered. "Subtlety is not his strong point." She turned away. "Let's get this done and get out of here."

"Absolutely," Luke agreed. "You take the computer. I'll take the wall."

Mandy looked at him quizzically. Why bother checking out the sick images he'd pasted to the wall?

"It's just the kind of stupid-clever thing Quentin would do," Luke explained. "Like those TV aliens. Hide a clue right out where everybody can see it."

"Right," Mandy agreed. Luke could see she was glad to take the computer. Not that it was any picnic. Most of Quentin's CD-ROMs were video games. The bloodier the better.

Luke went over the collage carefully, looking for a pattern. But the only thing the images seemed to have in common was their grotesque hideousness.

Nowhere did he find a whole human. All of the people were mutilated.

"Luke, look at this." Mandy sounded excited.

He joined her at the computer, desperate for some hope.

Mandy clicked on a file labeled UFO. Luke watched anxiously as Mandy paged through it, his eyes racing down the screen. But it was nothing more than a lot of downloaded junk from the Internet. Stuff from looney Web sites, none of which seemed to have a clue about what was *really* going on.

Mandy slogged through the whole file and they didn't learn a thing.

A car went by. Luke's heart skipped. A lot of time had passed. His pulse began to trip with anxiety.

"I haven't found a thing," Mandy griped, her voice tight.

"Me neither," Luke said. His eyes moved desperately around the room. "I know he's got something hidden here. I know it."

Luke started opening drawers. Mandy turned to the desk and grabbed a sheaf of papers.

A floorboard creaked somewhere. Their eyes jumped together, reflecting fear.

Luke turned back to the bureau, working feverishly. He hated touching Quentin's clothes. His skin crawled as though the contact was contaminating him.

Mandy made a small bleating noise. Luke whirled, adrenaline pumping.

Mandy leaned against the desk, her face pasty. A pile of pictures slipped from her nerveless fingers. Luke stooped to gather them up.

His throat closed at the sights which met his eyes. Mutilated animals. Strange deformities. Shaved dogs hooked to electroshock machines. He shoved the pictures in a drawer and got to his feet.

"Let's get out of here," he said gruffly. "There's nothing."

Mandy swallowed. "He must have given up on looking for us now," she said. Her voice was breathy, almost shrill. "He could be back any second."

"I was so sure we'd find something," Luke said dejectedly as they shut the door behind them. Evil seemed to leak out, even through the closed door.

They headed downstairs. Contradictory emotions bubbled through Luke's veins. Disappointment and horror, disgust and fear. But worst of all was the relief. He wanted to get out of the house, even though they hadn't found anything.

Mandy was about to open the back door when Luke stopped her.

He was staring at another closed door. Every nerve in his body was screaming to get out of this house. "The basement," he said, forcing the words out.

The dismay in Mandy's face echoed the dread curdling heavy in Luke's stomach.

But the basement was their last chance. They had to check it out.

With Mandy close on his heels, Luke opened the door to a black hole. The light switch at the top of the stairs didn't work. He started down, feeling his way. The stairs creaked loudly in protest.

Mandy followed, her breath sounding fragile.

Cold sweat broke out on his forehead. His chest felt tight.

Luke could feel the weight of the house closing in over his head.

He found a light switch at the bottom. A dim bulb illuminated an ordinary basement divided in half. One half was a workshop and laundry. They barely glanced at that.

The door to the other half was closed. On it was another sign:

PRIVATE!

KEEP OUT!

THIS MEANS YOU!

"Gotcha," Luke said softly. The door was locked.

"No problem," he told Mandy, pretending confidence. "It's just a button lock. My brother used to lock himself in the bathroom when he was little. I'm an expert at these."

He took out his pocketknife and fiddled with it. Sweat dripped in his eyes. He kept hearing noises from upstairs. Car doors. Footsteps.

"Luke. Listen!" Mandy had her ear pressed to the door.

Keeping his small blade in place, he leaned in closer. Faint noises came from the other side of the locked door.

Scratching sounds. Quiet, furtive noises.

Waiting. Eager.

The lock snapped.

Luke stared at the door. Fear whistled through him. Silently, on oiled hinges, the door swung inward into darkness.

A rank smell of rot — and something worse — rushed out.

Luke and Mandy staggered back, gagging. The noises were increasing in intensity.

Scrabbling. Crackling. Gnawing.

Fighting nausea, they knew they had to go in. Mandy held her nose, her eyes watering. Luke stepped inside, feeling for a light switch.

He snapped on the light.

At first he just stood rigid, shocked, struck dumb.

With a gargling noise, Mandy stuck her fists in her mouth to stifle her screams.

Chapter Thirty-four

The walls of Quentin's basement hideaway were alive with rats and roaches.

The creatures were in aquarium tanks, lined up on shelves. The shelves were stacked all the way to the ceiling.

There were hundreds of sleek black rats. Millions of large, fat cockroaches, some more than an inch long.

The rats were crowded, climbing over one another, scrabbling with their little claws at the glass walls. In the corners of the glass tanks, some lay still — probably dead.

The roaches covered the floors, walls, and ceilings of their tanks, a quivering mass of moving insect parts.

There was nothing else in the room aside from a bucket marked RAT FOOD and another marked ROACH FOOD.

Mandy took in little whimpering breaths,

trying not to breathe too much. The stench was overpowering. Apparently, Quentin didn't bother cleaning out the tanks much.

Beside her, Luke had seemingly turned to stone.

Once she got her stomach under control and the waves of revulsion stopped shuddering through her body, Mandy realized how disappointed she was.

But what had she been expecting? A clearly marked map tacked up on the wall? *This way to the spaceship.* Yeah, right.

A car stopped in the street outside. Luke gripped her arm. Mandy's heart seemed to stop.

Her eyes darted around the room, searching for a way out. But the only window was boarded over.

There was no sound of the front door opening. Maybe it was a neighbor.

Were the windows in the other half of the basement boarded up, too? She couldn't remember. Trying to picture what she'd seen in their quick look around, Mandy suddenly had an idea.

"Luke," she whispered. She cocked her head as if it was too dangerous to speak. Luke followed her out.

They stopped at the foot of the stairs and listened. There was still no sound upstairs.

Mandy gestured at Luke to follow her into the workroom in the other half of the basement. She sucked in her breath, a faint hope flickering inside her.

Luke pointed at the windows. There were two, and neither was covered with boards. "We can get out that way if we have to," he whispered.

Mandy nodded. Then she pulled him over to a shelf crammed with lawn-and-yard chemicals. "Look at this," she said eagerly, forgetting to whisper. She took down a large box and read the label.

"It's slow-acting rat poison. 'Guaranteed,'" she read. "'Acts slowly, forcing mice and rats to leave your house in search of water.' We could add it to the rat food."

Luke's eyes showed a glimmer of excitement. "Yes! Maybe the aliens will eat the rats before they die. It probably won't kill *them* but it will certainly make them sick and slow them down."

"Even if the rats die first," Mandy said, "it will reduce the aliens' food supply."

Luke scanned the shelf. "Here's another," he said excitedly, reading the label, "'Ants and roaches swallow the bait and take it home to the colony.' Perfect!"

"We've got nothing to lose anyway," Mandy pointed out.

They took the poisons back and hurriedly mixed them in with the food Quentin had ready.

It was more essential than ever to get out without Quentin knowing they had been here.

"Now what?" Mandy asked when they were done and Luke was relocking the door. "We still don't know where the ship is."

"We could kidnap Quentin and force him to tell us," Luke suggested halfheartedly as they hurried upstairs, both yearning mightily to get out of the house.

As frightening as the thought was, Mandy considered it. Then she shook her head. "These magnets work great. But I don't think we should risk getting that close to him. He might figure a way to beat the magnetic force if we gave him half a chance."

"I wasn't really serious," Luke admitted. "I don't think we could make him talk anyway. We don't have the right stomach for it."

They shut the basement door behind them. At that instant, a key turned in the lock of the front door.

A panicked glance flashed between them. They raced for the kitchen.

Mandy skidded across the tiled floor. Luke reached past her and grabbed the doorknob.

The front door opened.

"Hold it!" Quentin yelled. An order.

Chapter Thirty-five

Mandy froze.

Luke jerked open the back door.

"Wipe your feet," Quentin snapped to one of his skinhead followers. "Those boots are filthy."

Luke felt his blood start to pump again. Mandy dove through the door. Luke closed it behind them.

They huddled together, pressed against the house.

"It wouldn't have been such a great kidnapping opportunity after all," Mandy whispered, "unless you wanted to grab his skinhead gang, too." She was grinning shakily. Her eyes sparkled.

Luke was amazed at her cool. Then he noticed she was shaking as bad as he was. His knees were knocking so hard, he almost couldn't stand. Mandy was sliding down the shingled side of the house.

He lifted his chin toward the corner of the house. "Let's move around the side. Even if there aren't any bushes to hide under, at least there aren't any doors along there. There's less chance of being surprised."

Mandy nodded her agreement.

Luke slipped along the wall cautiously. Under the kitchen window he paused, listening for voices from inside.

He heard Quentin, but couldn't make out the words. His voice was gruff-sounding, angry. Then it came closer. Luke ducked farther below the window.

"So far you've failed to do the only thing I've asked you to do," Quentin complained acidly. "How do you expect to be warriors for the future? You can't even catch a puny girl and her half-wit boyfriend."

Luke couldn't tell how many skinheads were with him. They didn't make a sound.

"Jeff," Quentin barked. "Billy."

Luke jumped at the sound of his brother's name. His heart flopped like a dying fish. Maybe it was some other Jeff.

"Downstairs," Quentin ordered. "The rest of you jerks stay here."

Mandy poked Luke and together they scurried around the corner of the house. They crouched down by one of the unboarded basement windows.

Luke heard the door to the rat cave unlock. "Oh. Wow."

Luke's heart sank. That was definitely his brother. There were retching sounds.

Quentin laughed contemptuously. "I think you might be as lily-livered as your brother."

Mandy shot Luke a surprised look of sympathy. She had only just realized it was his brother down there.

"What you want us to do?" It was a different boy's voice. Sullen but willing.

"Two handfuls of that food for each of the rat cases. One of the other for the roaches. We'll be transporting all of them. The food makes them sluggish, easier to carry." Quentin chuckled. "And the dyzychs like the piquant flavor of half-digested food pellets in the soft gut. Helps make 'em crunchy."

His voice turned hard. "Buck up, Jeff. We haven't got all day. Unless you want to join your brother when this is all over. It won't be a pretty fate, believe me."

Luke thought of the mural up in Quentin's bedroom with the cartoon images of death. He pictured the skinheads on the gurneys with their skulls in a bowl and their bones pulverized. Quentin didn't have a pretty fate in mind for *anyone*.

Once all the rats and roaches were fed, Quentin summoned the rest of his gang. "Load 'em up, boys," he said. "You'll have to pack them full."

Luke and Mandy peered in the basement window but they couldn't see much. Except for an occasional groan of disgust, the skinheads were quiet as they emptied the rats into large backpacks fitted with animal carrying cases.

"You want the rewards, you gotta do the work," Quentin reminded them several times. He seemed to be moving from one to the other, inspecting their packing technique.

Once the rats were packed, he had them dump the roaches into canvas sacks and carry everything upstairs and out into the backyard. There were about a dozen skinheads helping him.

Luke and Mandy edged along the side of the house as far as they dared. The sun was beginning to set.

In the graying light, the black clothing and metal studs gave the skinheads a sinister but unreal look, like a tacky horror movie.

"They move like zombies," Mandy whispered.

Luke looked closer. She was right. There was an odd mechanical stiffness to most of them. "Quentin has them mind-controlled," he breathed. He didn't know if this made him feel better or worse about Jeff.

"Strap your packs on," Quentin ordered.

They all bent in unison, except for the two meanest-looking boys. Their movements were more natural. No hypnotism needed.

"They're squirmy," the biggest kid complained. The one with HATE scrawled across his forehead. He paused, scowling darkly, one arm through the strap.

Despite the heat, he wore a long-sleeved black shirt. His arms, boneless, bent oddly. None of the other boys seemed to notice.

But there was a shiver of tension in the air when he spoke. Everything stopped. The other kids looked expectantly at Quentin.

Luke felt a quiver of excitement. Quentin was having trouble controlling a group this big.

In two strides Quentin was in the big kid's face. "Put it on," he growled.

The skinhead, almost half a foot taller, stiffened. Then he ducked his head and shrugged the backpack on. "I was just saying," he whined. The tension was broken.

Quentin stepped back, surveying his gang closely. "Soldiers sometimes have to do grunt work," he said in a flat voice. "But this is the last time. After tonight, you'll each have more slaves than you know what to do with."

Several of the boys grinned back at him wolfishly.

Luke and Mandy exchanged a horrified glance. A vein in Luke's head began to pound.

"Hey, Q, this was a pretty cool idea," one of the smaller kids said. He wore lots of metal studs, but no tattoos. "Feeding the aliens rats and making them think it's real food. And they think they're better than us," he sneered, looking at the others for approval.

A couple more boys nodded and spit on the ground.

But Quentin was not amused. He yanked a fat rat out of the nearest pack. "This," he said, holding it up, "is an all-organic grain-fed farm-animal. Better food than any of you are used to."

Luke held his breath, thinking Quentin was going to make the kid eat the rat. But after a few seconds, Quentin returned it to the pack.

"He's afraid to test their loyalty again so soon," Mandy whispered.

Luke heard a note of optimism in her voice. He knew that she was grasping for hope.

"Each of you tie a sack to your belt and fall in," Quentin ordered.

There were some grimaces and mutters, but each of the skinheads picked up a sack of roaches as instructed.

Almost too late, Luke realized they would be marching around the side of the house. Without a second to spare, he and Mandy raced ahead of them.

They dove behind some evergreens planted

up against the front of the house. It was thin cover. Luke's hand sought Mandy's.

The blood in his veins turned to ice as the booted steps approached. The rhythmic noise pounded in his skull. If even one of the skinheads glanced sideways, he and Mandy would be caught.

The first ones passed. They marched in twos, side by side, faces forward. Their shaved heads gleamed dully in the growing darkness.

Luke stopped breathing. He hunched in on himself, trying to get smaller.

Quentin brought up the rear. Mandy gripped Luke's hand tightly. Surely Quentin could smell their fear.

But he was concentrated on controlling his "soldiers."

The skinheads hit the street. Boot heels echoed loudly on the pavement. A man watering his lawn looked up. He hurriedly shut off the hose and disappeared inside his house.

Luke and Mandy waited until the group had disappeared around a corner. Then they dashed down the street after them.

"Careful," Luke said when they reached the corner.

"We can't afford to lose them," Mandy answered, her voice tight. "This is our last chance."

"We can't afford to get caught either," he warned.

Although the night was dark, they would be easy to spot. It was the dinner hour. The few people who were outside retreated into their homes at first sight of the gang of skinheads walking in military formation.

The menacing chorus of marching boots was the only sound in the still air.

Avoiding streetlights, Luke and Mandy raced from shadow to shadow. It was soon obvious that Quentin was headed up Old High Street. He passed under the power lines without pausing.

A short distance later, the group made a sharp turn into the woods. Boots muffled by the soft ground, they instantly disappeared.

Alarmed, Mandy sucked in her breath. Together, she and Luke broke into a pelting run. Overhead, the power lines buzzed furiously.

Luke felt his veins constrict as sparks rained down on the road in front of them. But he and Mandy didn't falter.

"Was it here?" Mandy asked, searching the ground frantically.

"No," Luke said farther along the road. "Over here. They're headed toward the quarry. I remember this path. My brother and I used to take it years ago."

They hurried, going too fast for the darkness

and the uneven ground. The path was over-grown. Broken bushes snapped underfoot. The soft ground was churned up by the skinheads' heavy boots.

Running, Mandy stepped into a shallow de-pression. Her ankle twisted. Reaching to catch her, Luke caught his toe on a root. They both went down.

The noise seemed deafening in the stillness. They froze. But no one had heard.

Mandy scrambled up. "Let's go. They're way ahead of us."

Luke saw the wince of pain that crossed her face. The ankle was injured.

"I'm fine," Mandy insisted, trying not to hob-ble as she hurried on.

But Luke worried. They might need every ounce of speed.

"Maybe you should stay back, Mandy," he said as the woods thinned. "If I get caught, you can go for help."

She shot him a look. It was too dark to see her face, but he didn't need to. "We stick to-gether," she said.

Soon they were out of the trees. Luke hadn't seen the back end of the limestone quarry in years.

"Jeff and I used to play here," he said. "There are caves just big enough for a small boy to hole up in."

In the play of cool light from the crescent moon, the landscape looked desolate and spooky.

Nothing grew. Rock jutted up in low cliffs, rounded formations, and boulders.

Nothing moved.

"Where are they?" Mandy cried softly. "They can't just disappear."

Luke strained his ears while his eyes scanned every shadow. His mind was working at something. Something he'd forgotten.

"We'll have to backtrack," Mandy suggested. "They must have taken a turn in the woods that we missed. Nothing could hide out here."

Luke nodded. They started back into the trees. The ground was hard, just a thin layer of dirt over limestone. But even so, they could see that people had passed this way recently.

Passed out of the woods and vanished.

Mandy's shoulders slumped in defeat.

Then Luke remembered what was nagging at him. "Remember when I found that bit of clear stuff and chased the alien through the woods?"

Mandy winced. He knew she was recalling how she hadn't believed him.

"When the dyzych zapped the evidence, what was left was limestone dust," Luke said with growing excitement.

"So you think they're in there," Mandy asked

slowly, turning to look over the bare rocky terrain, "burrowed into the rock."

"There's got to be an entrance," Luke said. "No matter how concealed it is, there's sure to be dust. I wish we had a flashlight."

"This place is huge," Mandy said. She sounded miserable. "Whatever they're planning, it's going to happen tonight. We'll never find it in time."

"Most likely, the entrance is near here," Luke guessed. "Otherwise we would have seen Quentin when we came out of the woods. They weren't that far ahead."

"You're right," Mandy said, energy returning to her voice. She started toward the nearest humplike formation. "Let's hope they all have a nice big organic, grain-fed dinner," she added venomously.

"Remember, Luke," Mandy went on in a different tone, "no heroics. We find the entrance, we get out of here. Get help. We'll have no trouble being believed if we have an alien spacecraft to show."

"Believe me, I don't want to be a hero," Luke assured her.

It was slow going, searching in the dark for a certain pile of rock dust in a place full of rock dust.

Luke felt agitation building up in his chest. It was getting late. They were going to fail.

Luke heard a sound. A whooshing noise. Like bat wings, but bigger.

It flashed through his mind that he hadn't heard any normal night noises since they'd set out from Quentin's. As if all the animal life had fled.

Suddenly there was a flick at the edge of his vision. A dark swooping shadow. A black stain against the rock.

Mandy. Luke jerked his head. Where was she?

His pulse began to thrum ominously. "Mandy?" Quietly. Afraid to shout.

He heard a small noise. A cry. Pain, surprise.

"Mandy!" This time he shouted.

His voice bounced among the rocks. He shouted again.

The night closed in around him, thick as velvet.

Mandy was gone.

Chapter Thirty-six

Mandy paused to rub her throbbing ankle. As she bent over, a faint gleam caught her eye. Moonlight was striking something shiny.

She looked and it was gone. She moved her head slightly, side to side. There.

Keeping her eye trained on the faint glimmer, she started up a smooth slope. She dropped to all fours so she wouldn't slip.

There was a flutter of wings, but it didn't register. In the back of her mind, she heard a sound like a million soft-bodied moths. But she was intent on reaching the shiny beacon.

She crawled up to it and put out her hand wonderingly. Her fingers touched a smooth seam in the rock, dusted with fine powder. Almost invisible.

She stood up to find Luke. She didn't dare call out. Squinting into the darkness, Mandy felt the pressure swelling in her chest. Where was he?

A shadow passed. Dropped over her. A pulse of air on her arms. Before she could move, she was pinned. A coil wound smooth and hard around her body.

"Sorry," a soft, husky voice whispered in her ear, "but Quentin wants you."

Mandy gasped for air, trying to scream. But the coils tightened, squeezing the breath out of her. Nothing escaped but a shrill squeak.

The rock seam split. Darkness bled up into the night.

Fury poured strength into Mandy's muscles. She struggled, twisting and squirming. Her lungs screamed for air. The sinewy coils pressed, crushing muscle against bone.

Mandy felt something fall, little weights striking her foot, bouncing soundlessly to the ground.

Her magnets.

Loss swept through her, sucking the fight out of her mind.

The rock seam closed. Mandy was inside. A faint light emanated from deep within the rock. The coils loosened.

"What Quentin wants, Quentin gets." The soft voice sounded regretful.

Mandy staggered back and faced Cassandra. The woman smiled crookedly. Her long boneless arms rippled as she drew them in. "They — we — need him, you see."

She sounded sorry, which scared Mandy worse than anything. "Why?" she asked.

Cassandra considered her. "Why do you care? It's all over for you. I'll make your suffering brief." She sighed. "If I can. Maybe it will help to tell you that your sacrifice may spare humanity from extermination." She hesitated. "Not Greenfield, but most of Earth."

Mandy's insides turned to liquid. "What have *I* got to do with it?" she asked, her voice faint.

"Quentin is the only one who can detect the coming of the Others," Cassandra said with some distaste. "The dyzychs cannot live on Earth. They only want to enslave its inhabitants, to mine its mineral riches. The Others want the planet for themselves. They intend to wipe out the human population. And the dyzychs, of course."

Cassandra lifted a serpentine arm, nudging Mandy. "Come."

Mandy flinched away.

Cassandra laughed drily. "My touch is the least of your worries."

Mandy started along the stone passageway toward the light. As the glow grew stronger, the cold knot in her chest drew tighter. The passageway forked.

Cassandra directed her to the left. Mandy

stopped, swaying on her feet. She put her face in her hands, pretending to be overcome. Only an effort of will made it a pretense.

She dug her fists into her temples. While Cassandra stood patiently, Mandy pulled a few strands of blond hair from her head. She let some fall.

When the passageway forked again, she did the same. Then a sudden intensity of light blinded her. She had an impression of silvery metal rising high above her. The ship.

"Ah, Mandy."

Quentin's voice struck like a sharp blow. "I can smell your fear — a delicious aroma," he added as Cassandra led her through an open hatch into the brilliant light.

Mandy had expected another lab room, but this was different. It was furnished Earth-style. Dominating the room was a large bed.

"Welcome to my world," he said.

A shudder started deep inside her and enveloped her whole body.

Quentin's triumphant stare burned her skin wherever it touched. Something unnameable but powerfully dangerous radiated from him. Mandy felt it dissolving her will.

Then Quentin switched his attention to Cassandra. Mandy felt weak with relief.

"Where's the other one?" he demanded. "The stupid boyfriend."

"I had to grab her sooner than I planned," Cassandra reported. "She had found an entrance. Luke was too far off for me to get him at the same time."

"What?" Quentin's head swiveled toward a dyzych standing in another door, one that opened into the interior of the ship. Mandy had not even noticed the alien. "I thought it was supposed to be impossible to detect an entrance."

"Luke won't find it," Cassandra assured him. "It was the merest accident that she did. He's not looking in the right way."

"Not that it matters," Quentin said irritably. "Our work will be completed tonight."

He was interrupted by a dyzych carrying a steaming tray. The alien set it down on the table beside Quentin. The aroma, something like wet fur and hot, dirty socks, turned Mandy's stomach.

The dyzych lifted the cover. It was rat, skinned but still recognizable. Cockroaches, sluggish but not dead, garnished the plates.

Disgusting as the food was, Mandy felt a prick of excitement. In a few moments Quentin and his dyzych friends could be writhing in poisoned pain on the floor.

Quentin chose the largest plate. The serving alien handed another to the silent dyzych in the doorway and the last to Cassandra.

She smiled and waved it off. "I've become a vegetarian," she said.

Quentin shot her an irritated glance. Then he turned to the serving dyzych. "Has the gassing begun?" he asked.

The alien chittered and Quentin looked satisfied. He wafted his hand dismissively in Cassandra's direction. "Then get Luke now. I've waited this long, I want everything perfect. And that means Luke the Puke must be here to watch me enjoy what he never will."

Mandy's mind shut down. There was no longer room for any thought but that of escape. She lunged for the door.

Cassandra whipped out an arm, but Quentin stopped her. "No," he commanded.

Mandy reached the door.

"Mandy," Quentin barked. "Stop."

Instantly, every muscle in her body seized up. Her body was rigid but her momentum carried her forward.

She saw the floor coming up to meet her. But she couldn't raise her arms to break her fall.

Mandy shut her eyes.

Cassandra caught her inches before her face hit the metal floor.

Quentin laughed. "You're too sentimental," he told Cassandra. "It's a weakness."

"That's me," Cassandra answered bitterly.

She propped Mandy's rigid body in a corner. "Sentimental."

Cassandra went out to fetch Luke. Quentin turned his full attention on Mandy. An icy desolation blew through her, whistling out hollow bones.

Quentin eased back in his leather armchair, swinging his leg indolently. Quickly, he bit into the rat.

A smile twitched over his lips as he chewed. With every crunch of his teeth, he crawled a little farther into her brain. He was taking his time, reveling in her horror.

To Mandy, the creeping invasion was like a killing tide, poisoning everything it touched on its slow, unstoppable rise. Inside herself, she scrambled for higher ground.

But the evil blackness rose, lapping at her feet, then higher.

In her mind, Quentin watched, fascinated, as she was engulfed.

"Shall I tell you what we are doing?" His glee fed her fear, like gasoline dripped on a smoldering fire. "The dyzychs have created a heavier-than-air gas." He laughed, and spurts of flame seared the inside of her mind. "No, not poison. A sleeping gas."

He popped a roach inside his mouth, crunched. "Once the doltish population is unconscious, my loyal army of skinheads will be unleashed."

Quentin's eyes bored into her intently. "I'm sending them to your house first, Mandy. They will be armed. With a tool you are familiar with. I have christened it the Implant Gun. Your parents, and the rest of sleepy Greenfield, will dedicate the remainder of their lives to the dyzychs."

For an instant, Mandy forgot her own plight, overwhelmed by this new horror. It no longer mattered if Quentin and the dyzychs were all incapacitated by food poisoning. Quentin had won.

Quentin sighed dramatically. "Unfortunately, those lives will be brief. The nasty Others are coming, you see. The Others, sworn enemies of the dyzychs, cannot afford to let any dyzych slaves survive."

Quentin paused. In her mind, he projected a vivid image of blood, murder, and carnage. The Others, however, were only large shadowy forms.

"While the Others are busy wiping out Greenfield, the dyzychs will attack them. An ambush. Clever, isn't it? My idea, naturally." Quentin gnawed on a leg bone. "But you, Mandy my mate, will be safe with me. I have saved your life." He laughed. "And I expect the proper gratitude."

Mandy conjured up all the loathing she could and tried to spit in his face.

In reply, Quentin reanimated her body. He turned her toward the big bed. Flames licked the inside of her skin. She was burning up with his corrosive joy.

"*Don't worry, Mandy.*" Quentin's words were unspoken. They sounded only inside her head. "*I'm in no hurry. We have lots of time and I want to savor every second.*"

Mandy watched herself walk over, lie down. Her brain reeled. Her chest tightened. Yet her body breathed normally.

It was like there were two of her.

"I told you, Mandy"— Quentin spoke aloud this time, the words echoing a second time inside her head —"I don't need you willing. Just conscious."

He put down his plate. Stood.

Brown rat gravy dribbled down his chin.

Her revulsion invigorated him.

He came toward her. She scrambled desperately to escape.

But her body just lay there, inert and exposed.

Quentin's heat sucked oxygen from her lungs.

He bent over her, his grease-stained lips parted.

"Are you ready, my love? We'll start with a kiss."

Chapter Thirty-seven

Luke raced to where he had last seen Mandy.

He wanted to shout out her name again and again, but he knew it was no use. It would only bring the skinheads. Or the dyzychs.

He ran back and forth over the limestone formations, feet slipping, panic building. His head spun. How could she disappear without a trace?

His feet skidded on a sandy patch. His legs went out from under him and he landed on his tailbone. The pain traveled up his spine, leaving him gasping.

Luke knew he couldn't afford to hurt himself. He had to think. Maybe Mandy had found the ship.

Or maybe she had been captured before she could cry out.

Either way, the ship was here. Somewhere.

Luke cursed the darkness.

He tried to tell himself the darkness hid him. But as soon as he formed the thought, he felt eyes. The hairs rose on the back of his neck, down his arms.

His head swiveled. Nothing moved. All he could see was the desolate desert of rock.

But the eyes watched him.

His mind was playing tricks. Games he had no time for.

Shrugging his shoulders against the eery discomfort, he put the feeling out of his mind.

He crawled slowly over the ground, concentrating only on his task. His fingers explored every inch. He tried to imagine how Mandy would have gone about it. Luke pried at cracks, pressed his palm into depressions.

He looked for little piles of rock dust, imagining they might lie around like the excavations of ants.

And he kept his eye on the sky, remembering the bat-wind whoosh and the shadow he might have seen.

It was as he turned his head between Earth and sky that he saw the gleam. It was gone before he was sure he'd seen it. But Luke worked his way carefully in its direction.

The gleam didn't come again. His desperation was making him imagine things. Luke worked his jaw, his muscles rigid with tension.

He had to find Mandy.

He saw something dark wedged in a crack. He pried at it, but his finger was too thick. Out of the corner of his eye, he spotted an odd little pile of objects.

Dark things against the lighter limestone.

Crawling hurriedly, Luke kept his eyes trained. Unblinking, as if the objects might vanish before he could reach them.

His fingers closed over the small, black squares. Instantly he knew what they were. A chill settled over him. Mandy's magnets. Without them, she was helpless.

At the same time, his skin prickled with excitement. Now he knew where she had been. He ran his hands over the limestone, searching.

This was where he had seen the gleam.

Suddenly Luke paused. Mandy had disappeared. Lost her magnets. Something had been waiting here. Something had snatched her.

Without moving, he surveyed the ground and found a good-size rock. He took out his knife. Flattening himself against the rock wall, he twisted his head, looking for what Mandy had discovered.

Once his eyes picked up the tiny reflection, the hairline crack was revealed.

Stretching his arm full length, Luke ran his knife blade along the crack.

There was no sound.

But suddenly a yawning blackness appeared.

He felt the air behind him move an instant before he heard it.

The flap of giant bat wings.

Chapter Thirty-eight

Mandy frantically searched her mind for a way out. There had to be some way to get her control back.

But Quentin leaned slowly closer. His eyes looked like chips of filthy polar ice. But burning, too. Impossible. But they did burn.

Those eyes seared holes in her brain.

Quentin licked his lips.

Mandy's heart battered her ribs. Her skin broke out in goose bumps.

The tip of Quentin's tongue flicked out at her.

A chittering buzz suddenly came from the door.

Never had such an unpleasant noise sounded so wonderful to Mandy.

Quentin's face tightened in an angry snarl. His eyes snapped toward the door. "What is it?"

Mandy was still immobile. She couldn't turn

her head. But, strangely, she could see the dyzych through Quentin's eyes.

To her surprise, she realized Quentin viewed the aliens much as the dyzychs viewed humans. As a means to an end. With no significance in themselves.

The dyzych's answer affected Quentin profoundly. His anger blazed, but there was a peculiar stillness to it. Almost an uncertainty.

Abruptly, Quentin withdrew from her head.

"You're all sick? How can that be?"

The alien's answer trailed off in a sputtering hiss, like air escaping from a tire.

Out of the corner of her eye, Mandy could see the creature slump weakly against the doorjamb.

"Ridiculous," Quentin spat. "And impossible. I raised those animals myself. Besides, I probably ate more than any of you, and I'm not sick."

But a brief spasm crossed Quentin's face. Mandy felt his iron grip slip. Just a little.

She could move her head. But she didn't want to remind him she was there. Mandy tried not to breathe too much or even move her eyes.

Quentin strode toward the door. "If you dyzychs can't handle it, I'll get my boys to pump the gas. Without the sleeping gas, the plan has no chance. We'll be caught here like sitting ducks." A beat. "Or *you* will be, anyway," he added cruelly.

The dyzych bleated.

"Sitting ducks," Quentin repeated. "It means — oh, never mind." His voice faded as he hurried away down the hall.

Mandy felt herself slip back into her muscles and bones. She shook off the residue of Quentin's presence with a body-shaking shudder.

She sat up. The dyzych remained leaning in the doorway, looking weak and ill. Quentin had left it to watch her. Its big insect eyes turned slowly toward her.

The eyes were dull. The alien chittered weakly. Froth dribbled from its lipless mouth. It put up a hand. A warning probably. But its boneless legs collapsed under it like melting wax.

The dyzych slumped down the side of the door. It lay in a quivering puddle across the opening.

Mandy's mind worked feverishly. She had to get out of here.

She jumped off the bed. It would be no problem finding her way back to the entrance in the rock. Somehow she would get it open. Find Luke.

She started toward the door, eyeing the dyzych warily. She and Luke would come back into the ship. There was no longer time to go for help. But the aliens were incapacitated, or nearly so.

There was still a chance to beat them.

Mandy stepped over the dyzych quickly. It slowly lunged for her, but she easily evaded its reach.

The alien started to struggle upright. Mandy backed hurriedly down the hallway, keeping an eye on it.

She was almost at the first turn. Then an unfamiliar voice spoke behind her.

"Where do you think you're going?" It was a thin girlish voice. With an edge.

Before Mandy could turn, the long arms wrapped her like whipcord. Mandy glimpsed a tattoo on the boneless hand: LOVE.

Quentin's skinhead girl.

With a flick, the arms slammed Mandy against the limestone wall of the passage.

She heard her ribs crunch against the impact. Her breath was knocked out of her.

The skinhead girl was grinning. She no longer had a human face. The lipless mouth stretched grotesquely, exposing small, sharp teeth. Her skin was gray and rubbery. But it was her eyes that riveted Mandy's horrified attention.

"Humans are so breakable," the girlish voice said cheerfully. "The dyzych body is much superior."

Mandy sprawled on the floor. The Lucy-creature stood over her. Her faceted black in-

sect eyes glittered brilliantly even in the dim-
ness.

She grinned. "Q sent me to watch you." She
hauled Mandy to her feet and threw her back
into the room she'd so recently escaped from.

The sick dyzych dribbled and crawled into a
corner. It curled there, apparently unconscious.

"What happened to that one?" Lucy asked,
staring down at it.

Mandy felt a glimmer of hope. "I don't know.
Why don't you sit down. Have something to
eat. Quentin rushed off without finishing his
meal."

The Lucy-creature's eyes flicked toward the
half-eaten food. Her tongue slipped out between her small teeth. Then she took in the
room. "This is yours?" Her voice shrilled with
angry disbelief. "All I get is a capsule."

"It's not mine," Mandy said quickly. "It's
Quentin's."

Lucy suddenly advanced. Her arms flashed
in a blur. Mandy found herself knocked against
the wall.

"Q thinks he can still control me. He can't.
That's another advantage we human dyzychs
have." The alien eyes flashed cold fire. "I think
I'll leave him a little surprise. His special play-
thing, all cold and lifeless."

Mandy pressed herself against the wall. Her

brain scrambled. "Can't we talk about this? You can eat and we can talk it over."

"I already ate." Lucy advanced toward her, pinning Mandy with those awful eyes. "And after I strangle you, I'll eat again."

A wave of despair washed through Mandy. The rat and roach poison must not work on humans. Quentin, too, had seemed unaffected.

It was her last thought. Lucy's muscled fingers closed around her neck.

Mandy had never even seen the arms move, that time. She struggled to speak, but black spots danced before her eyes.

The spots swam together.

Mandy's sight dimmed.

Thought ceased.

Chapter Thirty-nine

Luke dove through the opening in the rock. Into blackness. In midair, he twisted his body and kicked.

His feet connected with something. He heard a pained grunt of surprise. As the stone door slid shut, he caught a glimpse of Cassandra sprawled on the rock. Outside.

Luke sprang to his feet and sprinted down the dim passageway. He knew he wouldn't have much time. As soon as Cassandra regained her breath, she'd be after him.

Adrenaline coursed through him. He came to a fork. He immediately turned right, never noticing the strands of blond hair scattered across the entrance to the other passage.

The stone hallway twisted and turned so that Luke soon lost all sense of direction. He began to worry as his heartbeat subsided slightly.

Where was the ship? Maybe he should go back, take the other fork.

But it made no sense to have a passage dug through the rock if it didn't lead somewhere. He kept going.

Rounding yet another bend, Luke stopped short. He was in a wide, low-ceilinged cavern. Filling the cavern was a gleaming, silvery ship like nothing seen on Earth.

It was round and low, but sleek. A faint humming noise came from it. Luke stared, awestruck.

Suddenly a deeper noise thrummed. It shook Luke from his trance.

Something was happening.

Cautiously he approached the ship, aware that a fast-moving dyzych could grab him before he even saw its shimmery presence.

But nothing stopped him. He did not even feel the eyes he had sensed outside. He was alone.

There was a hatch. With a tremor equal parts fear and confidence, Luke reached up and grasped what appeared to be a handle.

The hatch instantly swung wide.

Luke jumped, his heart in his mouth. The thrumming noise was louder. But nothing lunged out at him.

He hauled himself up into the opening. And almost fell backwards from fright.

The room was full of dyzychs.

Clutching the door frame, Luke steadied himself. Something was wrong. The aliens were lying on the floor, rocking feebly. Although their eyes turned toward him, they were dull.

He felt anger coming off them — and also helplessness. The poison had worked!

Energized, Luke sprang inside. He picked his way over the alien forms, toward the interior of the ship. His heart swelled with vengeful pride.

He would track the source of the sinister humming noise and shut it down. He would destroy the heart of the alien ship — the command module.

Then he would find Mandy. Together they would grab Quentin and force him to reveal the aliens' plans.

While confidence bubbled through his blood, Luke did not get foolhardy. He remembered his promise not to be heroic, and moved cautiously. He listened carefully.

He came to the big examining room. The one where they had operated on the skinhead girl. Empty.

Where had the human subjects gone?

Luke put it out of his mind. He reached the capsule room, which he thought of as the barracks.

It was crawling with dyzychs. Obviously, they had tried to reach their capsules. Most had failed and lay limp on the floor, barely moving.

But a few were inside the capsules. Luke paused, looking in.

The need to keep moving tugged at him. But he feared the aliens in the capsules. He knew they would be cleansing their bodies, recovering.

Forcing down his distaste and fear, he entered. An arm snaked toward his foot. But Luke easily saw it coming. He kicked the feeble limb away and stepped over the alien.

He drew out his knife and brandished it threateningly. Small as the blade was, none of the aliens seemed in the mood to argue with it. They let him pass.

But their eyes followed him. A breathy, hissing sound erupted from them when Luke cut the first hose.

He whirled, flicking his eyes, his knife ready. But no attack came.

Luke moved among the capsules, cutting the hose every time he found a dyzych occupant. It didn't take long. Most of them had collapsed right on the floor.

The hissing sound died as Luke picked his way back toward the entrance.

Going out, he shut the door behind him. He felt powerful.

"Take that, you loathsome aliens!" he yelled.

He passed the cafeteria. Dead rats lay on the floor and in the glass cages. Dead roaches littered every surface. Groaning dyzychs hardly noticed Luke go by.

It worried him a little that he wasn't finding any humans. No skinheads. No Quentin.

But the thrumming noise now filled his head. The floor under his feet vibrated, sending the unsettling sound up through his bones. It made his heart beat irregularly.

He had to make it stop.

Luke moved more quickly, almost jogging through the ship.

He knew now that the noise was coming from the command module.

And his luck was holding. The door was open.

Luke sidled along the wall. Peered inside. Two skinheads were pressing controls busily. One of them was the big mutant with the HATE tattoo.

The deep throbbing noise came from the big machine in the corner. It was a pump of some sort.

"Okay, pressure is up enough, finally," said the mutant. "Open the valve. Release the sleeping gas."

The mutant sounded so jubilant, Luke knew

it was essential to stop him. His eyes scanned feverishly for a weapon.

There were tools scattered over the massive pump. Several looked heavy enough to serve as clubs. But the mutant skinhead was standing too close.

The second skinhead — fully human — reached up to turn a round handle above a bank of computers. For the first time, Luke noticed the pictures on the screens.

They showed ordinary Greenfield streets. People sat on porches, enjoying the end of the mild evening.

The handle squeaked slightly as the skinhead turned it. The noise from the pump dropped. It settled into a steady pulse.

There was a moment of quiet. No one moved.

"Oowee, look at that," the human skinhead cried. "It works fast."

The mutant moved over to see the screen, his tattoo wrinkling with anticipation.

Luke seized his chance. He sprang at the pump. He grabbed the heavy tool, already spinning with it.

The mutant's arm snaked toward Luke with amazing quickness. But Luke had the momentum. The metal tool connected with the mutant's skull, and he went down like a stone.

The human skinhead's eyes were wide. He

backed up, feeling behind him for a weapon of his own.

Luke closed in, his blood hot.

There was a small sound behind him.

Instinctively Luke ducked. But not quick enough.

Rubbery arms closed around him.

Luke jammed his elbows backwards in a hard jab. He hit nothing but air.

And then he couldn't move at all.

"Grab some cord. Tie him up."

Luke was so shocked, the fight went out of him.

The voice was Mrs. Grundy's. She was speaking to someone in the hallway. "This darn whippersnapper's been trouble since the day he was born," she growled.

"I've got some. I'll do it." With a sinking pang, Luke recognized the second voice as well. Jeff.

Luke's arms were seized and roughly bound.

The mutant on the floor was beginning to stir. He sat, groaned, and fixed murderous eyes on Luke. His lips parted in a snarl as he started up.

"Leave him alone," Mrs. Grundy ordered, her skinny boneless arms waving like overcooked spaghetti. "Q wants this one for himself." Then she chuckled, a sound that rasped down Luke's spine like a rusty file. "Would you look at that. Amazing!"

On the computer screens, something strange was happening. A man slumped forward in a rocking chair. A woman reaching for a child suddenly fell to the ground. The child was already unconscious.

"I'll take him to Q." It was Jeff. His voice dripped with malice. "It will be my pleasure."

He gripped Luke's arm painfully just above the elbow. His eyes were dead above the spiteful grin.

Mrs. Grundy nodded absently. She was absorbed by the images on the screens. People dropping like flies.

"Hurry back," she said. "We have zombie slaves just waiting for us to come along and claim them." She turned to Luke. "The aliens cured my cancer. And now I'm going to live forever, with all of Greenfield to do my bidding." Her old face crinkled with glee. "Unlike you," she added and cackled.

Jeff joined in the laughter.

The sound pierced Luke like a viper's bite.

Chapter Forty

Red stars sparkled in amazing spirals against the black sky.

But how could the stars be red? Red as blood. Blood.

Something wasn't right.

Mandy heard a retching noise.

Light flooded the black sky. Her eyes sprang open.

The room whirled.

She was still in Quentin's awful room. The mutant girl Lucy lay on the floor, moaning, in a puddle of vomit.

Mandy's breath rattled in her aching throat. She scrambled to her feet.

Out of here. She had to get out of here.

There was movement in the corner. Mandy froze. But it was only the dyzych, comatose or nearly so.

Mandy started for the door. But as she

stepped over the alien's splayed legs, she heard footsteps. Running. Down the hall toward her.

Her heart sank. She had so nearly escaped.

Her eyes darted, looking for a place to hide. Under the bed. She shuddered.

The only other place was in the old-fashioned wardrobe. Mandy crossed the room and opened it. It was full of Quentin's clothes.

The smell of him — his Quentin stench — made her feel faint. It's only a smell, she told herself. She had to hide. Seeing Lucy and the dyzych, Quentin would assume she had fled. He'd go looking for her, and then she could escape.

Holding her breath, she climbed into the wardrobe. Her skin puckered at the touch of his things.

The footsteps stopped. "Mandy?"

She almost fell out of the wardrobe. "Luke!"

"What are you doing in there?"

"I thought you were Quentin," she said, throwing her arms around him.

She realized she had never done so before and felt a rush of happiness.

But fear bubbled just under the surface. "We've got to get out of here!" she urged, tugging Luke toward the door.

"Don't worry about Quentin," he said, pulling her back inside. "I've taken care of him. And everything else. I've stopped the dyzychs."

Mandy stopped, feeling disoriented. Luke's voice sounded flat, strained.

"I'm exhausted," Luke said. "Let's sit for a minute."

Exhausted, that explained it. Of course he was exhausted. "What did you do with Quentin?" she asked, marveling. Quentin had begun to seem invincible to her. A sort of perverted Superman.

"I'll tell you all about it. But first let me hold you."

He pulled her toward the bed. Mandy followed. She sat beside him, uneasily.

Luke pulled her close, almost roughly. Muscles jumped under her skin.

This wasn't like him. But he had just vanquished an alien race single-handedly. It was natural he'd be different after that.

"Wait, Luke," she said. "It's this awful room. I can't relax in here. Please, let's go."

"Maybe you're right. I know just the spot." Luke got up, keeping hold of her hand.

As Luke passed out the door, he looked back. Lucy was glaring suspiciously at him from the floor.

He winked at her. Quentin's wink.

Chapter Forty-one

Out in the hallway, Jeff maintained his vise-grip hold on Luke's elbow.

"Let me go," Luke whispered heatedly. "We're brothers, doesn't that count for something? Come on, Jeff. Snap out of it!"

But Jeff did not respond. It was as if he had been programed by Quentin.

As Luke struggled to get free, he tripped. As he fell, he saw alien eyes looking out of his brother's face. "Get up. We must obey," his brother said.

Luke threw himself at Jeff's knees, catching him by surprise. Jeff went down hard, smacking the back of his head on the floor with a dull thud.

Quickly Luke pressed his bandana-wrapped forehead against Jeff's, willing the magnets to work.

There was no response. Had he killed his own brother?

Then Jeff groaned and sat up, rubbing his head. "I'm back!" he gasped.

"What?"

"My head. Quentin must have hypnotized me or something. He had a lock on my mind. It was creepy. Like I was someone else." Jeff's eyes were undeniably his own, and that made Luke feel almost giddy with relief.

Jeff quickly untied the knots binding Luke's arms. "We've got to find some weapons and stop those guys. They're going to turn Mom and Dad and the whole town into slaves for the aliens."

"Where's Quentin?" Luke asked, his blood beginning to pump once again.

"He's —" Jeff's face drained of color. "He's got Mandy. She's supposed to join him on the ship. As his mate."

Luke's expression darkened. "You know where they are?"

Jeff shrank in on himself. "Yeah. But we can't go there. He'll get us both. We won't be any use with Quentin in our minds."

"He has no more power over us," Luke said. He pulled a couple of magnets out of his bandana. Stuck them in Jeff's pockets. "Keep these on you. I'll explain as we go."

Jeff looked doubtful, but he led Luke into the

back part of the ship and through a door Luke hadn't seen before. There was a short hallway. Light spilled from an open door.

Luke heard a groan. He broke into a run.

"Careful," Jeff whispered.

Luke paid no attention. He wasn't afraid of Quentin anymore. He ached to sink his fists into Quentin's soft belly.

But the room was empty. Except for a sick alien. And that poor mutant girl. She sat against the wall, arms wrapped around her stomach.

Luke slumped. He didn't know where to look next.

He didn't notice Lucy fix her cold insect eyes on his back.

Chapter Forty-two

Mandy's nerves prickled. "Why are we going this way?" she asked as Luke pulled her through the door that led into the ship. "If it's all over, can't we go out through the rock passage?"

"I want to show you what I've done," Luke said.

His gloating tone sent a shiver through her. Something was wrong here.

Suddenly she realized what it was. "Luke, where is your bandana?"

"My bandana?"

A jolt of alarm sizzled up Mandy's spine. This wasn't the Luke she knew and loved. Without the magnets, he was Quentin's robot.

She tried to keep her breathing steady. He must not guess.

Mandy forced a laugh. "Let go a minute. You're hurting my hand."

But his grip tightened. Mandy felt her mind go slowly numb.

"How did you guess?" Luke asked. "I thought I was doing so well."

But Mandy couldn't answer. She was locked away again, as quick as that. Her mind was crawling with horrors.

Luke opened the door to one of the examining rooms. "Upsy daisy," he said gleefully in Quentin's voice.

Mechanically, Mandy climbed onto the gurney. Her mind was screaming.

Luke pressed a button and a tool jumped to life, shrieking along with her.

"I've thought of a unique experiment," he said over the piercing noise of the tool. He held the tool out so she could see it.

It was a saw. Buzzing so fast it was a blur.

Portions of her mind blanked out.

"I thought I might remove the top of your skull." He grinned at her and bent to watch her eyes. He frowned. "You're not there, Mandy. We can't have you absent."

She felt a tingle of pain, like an electric shock passing behind her eyes. Instantly every nerve was alive. She could feel the blood flowing in her veins.

"Luke!" she screamed inside her head. "How can you do this?"

She knew Luke had no control, but her

eyes searched for him. What she found instead drained her last hope. She realized it wasn't Luke at all, but Quentin shaping himself to look like him. Which meant there was no hope for her. None at all.

"I'm going to remove the skull so I can watch what happens in the brain when I make you my mate," he said. "No one has ever determined if there is any actual physical response in the brain."

He shivered with delight and lowered the screaming saw.

Chapter Forty-three

A low, unpleasant laugh jerked Luke around.

Luke looked away after the dull black eyes met his. A vein quivered in Lucy's bulbous forehead.

"Quentin," she said in a weak raspy voice. "I know where he is."

Luke came to attention.

"He must have poisoned my food," Lucy gasped. "And now he's playing nasty games with that girl."

"Where?" Luke felt his throat closing with fear.

"He's going to make her like me." Lucy shrugged weakly. "Or maybe he's just going to cut her up. Whichever, he's in one of those rooms."

She slumped against the wall again, overcome by another fit of retching.

Luke set off at a run, retracing his steps. Jeff was right behind him.

"We need weapons," Jeff pleaded.

"All I need are my fists," Luke said, pounding down the hall.

He yanked open a door but the room was silent, the gurneys empty. Before he reached the next one, the shrill sound reached him.

He couldn't be too late. His heart constricted. Luke skidded to a stop, his noise covered by that piercing whine.

He looked around the edge of the door.

He saw himself. Lowering a medical-type saw onto Mandy's head.

"Stop!" he yelled, the sound torn from his throat.

His double wheeled around in surprise.

As Luke stared, the illusion melted away. Quentin snarled at him with an expression that was distinctly non-human. He held the saw close to Mandy's head.

"What are you going to do, big boy?" Quentin demanded, his voice booming.

Luke swallowed. He hardly dared breathe. The whirring blade was almost pressing Mandy's skull.

"Rush me and I plunge this nifty little tool right through her pretty head," Quentin taunted. "Oops, no more Mandy."

Jeff came up behind Luke and grabbed him roughly. He jerked him into the room. "Sorry, Q," he said in the flat voice Luke had come to dread. "He got away from me."

"Maybe it's better this way. Bring him closer," Quentin ordered. "I want to be sure he can make out the details."

Luke felt Jeff give him a nudge. He stayed stiff when Jeff let go. Jeff moved toward the gurney, his face slack, his hand in his pocket. "Can I watch, too?" he asked.

Quentin shrugged.

He bent over Mandy once again.

Then a shadow crossed his face. He winced, jerking the saw. It dipped, missing Mandy's head by a fraction.

Luke's heart skipped.

The presence in his brain wavered, uncertain.

Luke shot Jeff a look. It was now or never.

"Go, brother," Luke said.

Jeff threw the magnets onto the gurney.

"Hey!" Quentin said, startled, just as Mandy's hand jerked up and knocked the surgical saw flying. The blade skittered on the floor and then bounced up, catching Quentin on the ankle.

"EEEEEEE! EEEEEEEEE! EEEEEE-EEE!"

Quentin shrieked as a little green liquid

spurted from his injured ankle. His eyes began to glow with heat.

"Now you die!" he screamed.

Quentin leaped through the air, his hands turning into writhing tentacles that whipped around Luke's neck.

Luke felt the strength being drained from his body. The tentacles tightened, and he saw Quentin's head throbbing and pulsing, as if the alien creature inside was about to come out.

Quentin's mouth opened. His teeth had become fangs dripping with venom.

"Say good-bye, Lukie boy."

The tentacles were so tight that Luke felt nothing but pain. He couldn't even hear what Quentin was saying. The words sounded like a buzz or a whirr.

The whirr of the surgical saw.

"EEEEEEEEEEEEEEEEEEEE!"

An inhuman, high-pitched shriek was suddenly coming from Quentin. The tentacles suddenly released Luke. As he choked in some much needed air, he saw that Mandy was wielding the surgical saw.

She'd hacked off Quentin's tentacles. The slimy things writhed on the floor as if they had a life of their own.

"Too late!" Quentin shrieked as he collapsed, spewing more of the disgusting green liquid. "You still lose!"

Chapter Forty-four

Staring down at the revolting, badly injured creature, Mandy discovered she couldn't take pleasure in his defeat. Quentin had been a loser and a bully, but he'd once been human.

Jeff slumped to the floor, dejected. "He's right. We may have beat Quentin, but we're too late. Mom and Dad are zombies. And we're all going to be mutants, if they don't just kill us."

"Except for Mandy," the Quentin-creature taunted, gasping for breath. "She's going to be Mrs. Q. She's going to bear my children. Of course they won't be human children, will they, Mandy?"

"What's he talking about?" cried Luke. He was still sitting on Quentin, holding him down, although the badly injured creature had lost most of his strength. "Get me some cord," Luke said to Jeff. "We've got to tie him up."

"Don't listen to him," Mandy urged. "I know

what he planned to do. As soon as they finished gassing the town they were going to drop off the skinheads with implant guns, to make slaves out of everybody," she explained hurriedly.

As she helped tie Quentin up, he hissed and spit. "She lies! Untie me and I'll show you the truth!"

Mandy ignored him. "But invading the town was really only a diversion," she continued. "The Others are supposed to find the slaves, the humans, and wipe out Greenfield, giving the dyzychs a chance to set up an ambush."

Luke gaped at her. Jeff did, too.

Quentin cackled hideously. "You forgot to mention that the ingenious idea of an ambush was mine, all mine!"

Mandy ignored him although even the sound of his weakened voice roused murderous feelings in her. "So the plan is complete," she said. "The dyzychs are lifting off."

Luke jumped to his feet. "We've got to stop them."

"We'd better take him," said Jeff, indicating the tied and bound Quentin. "We need to keep him where we can see him."

Mandy ran on ahead to reconnoiter while Jeff and Luke carried Quentin. Dyzychs still lay in the hall and cafeteria, seemingly as sick as ever.

That puzzled her. How was the ship starting up without them?

Another blast of noise shook the spacecraft.

Light spilled from the command module. "Blasting system go," she heard.

In English. A woman's husky voice.

Cassandra.

"Come in, Mandy," she called with almost no change in inflection.

Mandy started. How had she known? She couldn't have heard her, not with all this noise. Mandy walked forward, her heart thudding painfully.

Inside, a pale dyzych worked beside Cassandra. Even as Mandy watched, it doubled over in pain.

Mrs. Grundy lay moaning in a corner. The other mutant and skinhead were gone.

"I have some mild talents of my own," said Cassandra, without looking away from her computer dials. "Nothing like Quentin's, of course, but they didn't know about him when they chose me."

She laughed, a sound as silvery as the dyzych garment she wore. "Just goes to show we all make mistakes, even the dyzychs." She raised her voice. "Come in, boys. I have good news. For some of you."

Luke and Jeff appeared, Quentin propped between them. He smirked. "Tell these puny creatures what lies in store for them," Quentin said, a spasm of pain crossing his face.

Mrs. Grundy raised her head, let out a horrible shriek like an angry cat. "You!" she screamed, pointing with a shaky, boneless finger. "It was you two troublemakers."

Luke realized she meant him and Mandy.

"You poisoned our food. You have been nothing but a nuisance since the day you were born." Another spasm shook her and Mrs. Grundy subsided back into a heap on the floor.

When he grasped what they'd done with the rat poison, Quentin looked at Luke with bleary-eyed hatred. "I should have guessed," he said, with outraged amazement.

Cassandra smiled, pressed another button. Another roar sounded.

"You and I will be departing this planet in a few minutes, Quentin," she said crisply. "These people will be staying. I have aborted the dyzych mission." She looked at Mandy. "The gas has been dispersed. No one will ever remember passing out."

"What?" Quentin's eyes bulged. He coughed and a spot of green slime appeared on his distorted face. "The dyzychs will have your liver out for that."

"I don't think so," Cassandra said confidently. "The dyzychs need us now more than ever. They are recovering, but without proper food they can't be expected to fight. You and I and a few of your half-breeds will be doing the fighting for them."

"Fighting?" Quentin sounded puzzled.

"Yes. After you and the dyzychs recover, we'll meet the Others in space and battle them there. As the dyzychs should have done from the start."

Cassandra pressed a button and a hatch opened. Outside the hatch it was night. The barren limestone landscape spread before them like the loveliest spot on Earth.

Cassandra looked at Mandy, Luke, and Jeff. "I've already freed Quentin's other stooges. The ones who were still human," she said. "You'll have to find a way to work with them if Earth is to survive. No one else will believe you. Now, go, please."

Quentin struggled against his bonds. "Let me out!" he demanded. "I'm human!" he cried desperately. "I'm better than human. I belong on Earth!"

"Sorry," Cassandra said. "You made your choice, Quentin. Now you'll have to live with it."

She turned to Luke and Mandy. "I wish I could say you'll be free of us from now on, but I'm afraid Earth is just too rich. The invaders will return."

Mandy tugged at Luke. She wanted out of

here before spooky Cassandra changed her mind.

Quentin remained on the floor, moaning and muttering to himself as his tentacle stumps quivered.

Luke reached for his brother's hand. They all stepped out of the spacecraft together.

"Whoever wins the war in space will return to Earth," Cassandra called out to them. "Be forewarned."

Luke put his arm around Mandy as the ship slowly lifted off. Mandy slipped her arm around his waist. She lay her head on his shoulder and watched the glistening spacecraft recede into the distance.

Luke thought he'd never had a better moment in his life.

"We'll beat them," Jeff vowed, shaking his fist at the sky. "We will."

With his other arm, Luke drew his brother in. For once Jeff didn't fight him.

The three friends stood together and watched the ship until it was only a tiny red dot in the sky.

"They'll be back," Jeff reminded them.

"And this time we'll be ready," Luke and Mandy said together.